BLACKMAIL

First Edition

Published by The Nazca Plains Corporation
Las Vegas, Nevada
2007

ISBN: 978-1-934625-47-7

Published by

The Nazca Plains Corporation ®
4640 Paradise Rd, Suite 141
Las Vegas NV 89109-8000

PUBLISHER'S NOTE
Blackmail is a work of fiction created wholly by the imagination of the authors named herein. All characters are fictional and any resemblance to any persons living or deceased is purely by accident. No portion of this book reflects any real person or events.

Cover, Vladislav Gansovsky
Art Director, Blake Stephens

DEDICATION

To Jeffrey and Dominick, best friends and family…

BLACKMAIL

First Edition

Edited by Christopher Trevor

CONTENTS

INTRODUCTION
A Brief History of the Word: "Blackmail"

"Blackmail" is the harrowing subject of this book, and perhaps there will be another following this series of sinister tales. In my opinion the word "Blackmail" can be enough to strike terror into the hearts of even the most powerful of men. As the editor of this book I can honestly say that I don't know what your individual experiences may be, but you would have no idea just how much blackmailing there is going on out there at this time.

Blackmail is the act of threatening to reveal information about a person, information that the person would not want revealed, or even do something to destroy the threatened person, unless the blackmailed target fulfills certain demands. This information is usually of an embarrassing or socially damaging nature.

In a broader sense, blackmail is an offer to refrain from any action which would be legal or normally allowed, and is thus distinguished from extortion.

The word "Blackmail" is derived from the word for tribute paid by English and Scottish border dwellers to "Border Reivers" in return for immunity from raids. This tribute was paid in goods or labor (reditus nigri, or blackmail): the opposite is blanche firmes or reditus albi, or "white rent" (denoting payment by silver.)

Also:

The word itself, "Blackmail" looks weird because we do not know the relevant meaning of the second part. It really has nothing to do with mail delivered by the postal carrier, which is from Old French male, for a wallet (the word transferred from the pouch carried by a messenger to the things carried in the pouch.) Nor is it linked to the chain mail of medieval knights; this comes from Latin macula for a spot or mesh, referring to the individual metal bits of the mail. (So blackmail, despite what you sometimes read, has nothing to do with medieval knight's chain mail turning black as ghastly retribution for dishonorable deeds.)

The mail in blackmail (at various times also spelled maill, male and in other ways) is an old Scots word for rent. This was usually paid in what was often called white money, as mentioned earlier, silver coins. It comes from Old Norse mal, meaning an agreement, later a contract, and then payment specified by the contract. In the sixteenth and seventeenth centuries chieftains in the highlands of Scotland and along the border between Scotland and England ran protection rackets in which they threatened farmers with pillage and worse if they didn't pay up. This amounted to an informal tax or extra rent and the farmers, with white mail that they paid. Black has for many centuries been associated with the dark side of human activities, hence blackmail.

The term was extended in the nineteenth century to other ways of extorting money with menaces, and in particular to the threat of exposing a person's secrets.

So there you have it, a brief history of the word "Blackmail." Please feel free (or perhaps not so free) to e-mail me your own harrowing tales of blackmail at "ExecSocks@AOL. com and we will gladly consider them for future publications.

Christopher Trevor

ROOM SERVICE
Chapter One
Written by: Tim Marks

Thomas was dead tired by the time he got back to the hotel. It had been a long day working out the final details of the Richardson merger, but it looked like they were very close to getting a deal. And that meant not only a promotion or even a partnership, but a very nice cash bonus as well. At 28, Thomas was already a shooting star in the investment bank, known for his pretty boy looks but ruthless ways. He had made some enemies on the way up, having to deal with untalented and unintelligent staff, but that came with the territory.

The Westin, he thought, as he went through the grand gilded lobby, was a fairly nice place to stay. Even after weeks away from home, he still enjoyed the exquisite service that the hotel offered, and by now, after three weeks here most of the staff knew his name and greeted him with respect and deference. Even the cute little elevator boy who took him downstairs every morning bowed and scraped when he appeared, dressed to kill in his expensive Armani suit and highly polished Alden shoes. Although Thomas was married and completely straight he liked having other males being subservient to him in an almost sexual way.

The door to the room did not open as easily as usual when he pushed in the key card;

11

It seemed somehow to be stuck. But a hard push with Thomas' fairly muscular shoulder made it give, and he wearily flung his briefcase and keys on the dresser before going into the bathroom to relieve himself, taking a minute to refresh his tired but still very handsome face in the mirror.

The bedroom seemed somehow darker to him when he came out again, but before he had time to think about it a large and powerful gloved hand was clapped over his mouth and what felt like a gun was stuck in his ribs. Thomas struggled to get away or at least see who his attacker was, but this man was bigger and stronger than he. And when the pad of wadded up paper with the sickly smell was pressed to his nose and mouth he knew he was in a lot of trouble indeed.

When he came to he found himself stretched spread eagle on the bed, arms and legs securely tied to the bedposts. His mouth was dry and pain-filled with what seemed to be his Calvin Klein underpants duct taped inside. He was still in his suit, but his T-shirt was ripped open and his pants were pulled down around his ankles. As he looked down, he could just see the words "Faggot" and "Ransom Me" written on his upper thighs in black Magic Marker.

Even though the room was still dim, Thomas could just make out a husky dark figure sitting in the desk chair, intently studying something. As the anesthesia began to wear off, the figure came into better focus. It was a fairly powerfully built man, dressed entirely in black and wearing a black ski mask. The object of his study was Thomas' wallet, and he seemed to be busy extracting business cards and writing down credit card numbers, pausing occasionally to sip from a stiff whiskey from the mini-bar at his side.

Thomas groaned to signal he was awake and his captor looked over at him. "Good evening, Mr. Sutton," he said. Alarmed that this stranger knew his name Thomas began to shake his head violently from side to side, but the gag kept him from saying anything intelligible. He had no idea how long he had been like this, or what this man wanted. But he was going to have to think fast and hard to negotiate his way out of this situation.

The stranger strolled over to the bed and handled Thomas' exposed and half-stiff cock in a familiar way. "That was quite a show you put on for me," he said, "You are even more of a faggot than I thought. Even unconscious, you did a great job giving me a blow job as well as some more fun. I got some great pics of it as well, want to see?"

Thomas shook his head furiously, but the stranger had pulled a digital camera from his pocket and began to show a number of shots of a drunk-looking Thomas, face clearly visible, with Cock in his mouth, legs spread for the camera with the writing on the thighs and finally another close-up of his business card propped up on his erect cock.

"If things don't work out at your present place of employment after this you can always get a job as a porn model," said his tormentor. Something about the man's voice and also his somewhat shuffling bearing as he crossed the room to fetch his drink seemed vaguely familiar to Thomas. More importantly, however, he had to find out how this man seemed to know so much about him, what he wanted and how he was going to extricate himself from this very threatening and compromising situation.

Thomas groaned and cried furiously through his gag, but this only seemed to amuse his captor. Finally, he came back to the bed. "I'll make a deal with you, Thomas," he said. "I will un-gag you so that we can have a conversation. If you yell out or are disrespectful in any way the gag goes back in and I walk out with your wallet and keys, as well as all the confidential contract briefs for the Richardson merger. Understand, big boy? Do we have a deal?"

Weakly, Thomas nodded yes and was rewarded and relieved when the tape was roughly ripped off and the underpants, smelling of urine he did not think was his, removed. He licked his dry lips and gratefully took a drink of the water offered him. This stranger was oddly solicitous, even in this situation, again reminding Thomas of some unrelated situation.

"I want to propose a deal to you, Mr. Thomas Sutton," said his captor. "I have gone to a lot of trouble to come visit you here this afternoon and I need to be compensated for that trouble. That process is going to have a couple of steps. First, I am going to need some cash from you. I have already helped myself to the $200 you had in your wallet, but I am going to need quite a bit more. So you are going to give me your PIN number so I can take care of that. After that, if that checks out, I will be back for a little recreational sex with you. Provided you satisfy me fully in that regard I will allow you to go back to your little wife, keeping all of this, as well as those nice pics I have of you our little secret. Now what do you say, big boy?"

His kidnapper gave his nipple a playful but also painful twist as he leaned over him. With his other hand, he reached down and squeezed his balls hard. The pain and humiliation were excruciating. "What is the number, faggot?"

Thomas stood it for a minute or so, but finally could take the pain no longer. "5857" he screamed into the room. The kidnapper stood up, went to the desk and wrote the number down. He then picked up the roll of duct tape, carefully stuffed the underpants back in Thomas' unwilling mouth and taped it shut. Then, several silk ties from his suitcase, knotted together, were tied around his head as a blindfold.

Thomas could hear the man moving around in the room, apparently changing clothes. Finally, he felt a suited knee hit his exposed crotch and caught a whiff of his expensive cologne. He heard a voice whisper in his ear "I'll be back in a little while, faggot. Don't go anywhere". And with that he heard the jangle of his keys and the click of the hotel room door closing. He was alone again, and completely helpless.

Chapter Two

Thomas woke up almost immediately as he heard the key turning in the door. His arms ached from being above his head for so long, and he desperately needed to piss. But most frustratingly he could feel that his cock was still half erect in between the obscene writing on his thighs. As outraged and afraid as he was at what was happening to him something inside of him was very turned on by this blatant demonstration of power and sexual domination. This man was even more sure of himself than was Thomas, and he had to respect that.

From the door, however, came not one but two male voices: his assailant was not alone! In a moment, the murmur from the hallway came into focus. "Wow, awesome!" said his new visitor, "holy shit!" He felt a pair of hands admiringly caressing his pecs, then his thighs, and finally whoever they were they grabbed his cock, which instantly sprang obediently to attention.

"How are you doing, Mr. Sutton?" asked the voice, already familiar from the ordeal earlier in the afternoon. Thomas struggled violently, and grunted, begging for the gag to be removed. Thankfully, surprisingly, he felt a rough pair of hands ripping off the duct tape and extracting the piss-soaked briefs from his mouth. Licking his dry lips, he croaked: "Please, I have to pee".

"Is that a full sentence, faggot?"

"I have to pee, Sir, please, Sir!"

Thomas could hear the visitor snickering at this humiliation, but that shame was soon overwhelmed with relief as his bonds were loosened and his hands then swiftly handcuffed behind him. Slowly, groggily, he sat up, well aware that blindfolded, handcuffed, with two Men now guarding him, he was scarcely in a better position than before. Escape was impossible, and resistance definitely not a good idea.

"Okay, faggot," said the voice, "crawl on into the bathroom and do what you have to do. But leave the door open, and keep in mind that fags piss sitting down." Thomas nervously kicked off his expensive wingtip shoes and tried to straighten his suit pants, then dropped to the floor and crawled laboriously to the bathroom, feeling his way as he went. He heard his two visitors laughing uproariously at his progress.

When he came out, relieved but very embarrassed, he heard the sound of glasses clinking: his visitors were having drinks from his mini-bar. Desperately, he tried to retreat into the corner, but a rough hand grabbed his hair and forced his face into the light.

"Cute, isn't he?" said the voice.

"Holy shit, isn't that the executive hotshot who has been pushing us all around for the last few weeks?" inquired the visitor. "This asshole stiffed me when I served him his breakfast this morning!"

In a flash, Thomas realized: this tormentor was one of the Latino breakfast waiters in the hotel, the ones he had indeed never thought of tipping in all the weeks of eating breakfast here. And now this low life scum was seeing him in this position! Angry, frustrated and helpless, he started to cry.

"Turn around, faggot, and show my buddy your fuck hole!" said the first voice. Terrified, he numbly did as he was told, and felt the suit pants pulled down again, along with the boxer shorts, exposing his naked ass to inspection. "Very nice," said the visitor, "this faggot's ass is even nicer than we thought. My buddies and I have been admiring it for weeks under the fancy suit."

"Do you want a piece of it?" asked his first captor.

"Nah, that's ok, but I could do with a blow job before I go on the evening shift".

"Sure thing, bud, just give me a minute to get things set up."

Thomas heard some odd clicking and rummaging around before the order came.

"Crawl over and suck my buddy's cock, faggot. You better do a good job if you want to keep your big job and your little wife."

Totally amazed at this turn of events Thomas stumbled blindly over in the direction of the visitor's voice. His mouth clumsily found his way to the visitor's crotch and discovered his pants opened and a big uncut dick already hard and waiting for service. Numbly, obediently, his mouth went down on it and, choking on the humiliation, did his best to suck rhythmically and get the visitor off as quickly as he could.

"Whoa, easy, faggot!" said his target, "no teeth!" A hard slap across his ass warned him to be more careful. Another sob escaped his lips as he obediently went down on the cock once more. What was he reduced to? Thomas Sutton, rising star at Gold Hightower Inc., now giving head to a lowlife breakfast waiter. But he saw no other option but to continue. These men were serious, and already in a position to destroy him if he angered them.

Thankfully, the waiter soon began to thrash around, then pulled out and jerked himself off, shooting all over his chest as well as Thomas' face and hair. Then, to Thomas' chagrin, his tormentor calmly began scooping up the cum from his chest and rubbing that into Thomas' hair as well. "Thanks, I needed that'," he said, patting Thomas on the head as he zipped up and prepared to go.

"Did you get it all?" the visitor asked the first captor.

"I think so, very hot indeed!"

Thomas turned his head like a deer in the headlights. "Right, faggot, you are a movie star! This video camera I just bought with your American Express card works great. And even with the blindfold on, it is clear that it is you. You are a natural cocksucker!"

Thomas sank to his knees, now sobbing uncontrollably, as he realized the enormity of what had just happened and the overwhelming power this stranger now had over him. Everything was at stake now, his job, his marriage, his financial stability – and all because of this Stranger and his unaccountable drive to humiliate him.

He hardly heard the door close behind the visitor when the order came to crawl over to the desk chair and sit down. Trembling, he did as he was told. This time, his suit pants and boxer shorts were pulled off entirely and his expensive silk shirt was ripped open and yet another word written on his chest in Magic Marker. New ropes were wrapped around his wrists and ankles and his torso was securely trussed to the chair as well.

"So, big boy, time to have a conversation," came the voice. The blindfold of knotted silk ties was removed, and the light of day returned to his eyes. As the room came into focus so did the leering face of his captor, seated comfortably in the other chair. Thomas gasped in recognition.

Chapter Three

Thomas scrunched up his eyes trying to see more clearly.

His room key was dangling in front of him, and behind it was a familiar face with a no longer respectful and now quite threatening leer:

"Number 546, Mr. Sutton?"

He had heard that phrase every day now for three weeks from the lowlife desk clerk downstairs, always with a subservient tone mixed with a little cockiness. Little more than a boy this scrawny little shit had consistently given bad service, and he had to let him have it more than once for keeping him waiting with the key and, once, losing an important fax that had come in from a major client. And now here he was in his room grinning insolently at him.

Thomas summoned his most authoritative manner. "Look, fellow, this has to stop. I am a guest in this hotel, and I demand that you respect that."

"Somehow you aren't as intimidating with "COCKSUCKER" written on your chest," was the insolent reply.

Thomas looked down to see that his tormentor was right. Under his ripped shirt and T-shirt the insult was scrawled prominently in red magic marker on his body.

In a flash, Thomas now understood how this man had so easily gotten access to his room, why he knew his name, and he shuddered to think what else he might have gleaned from the hotel guest records. There was no time now to think about how to get revenge on this brazen attack on his dignity, privacy and wallet, but he was puzzled that a mere desk clerk could dare to do this to a guest like him.

Swallowing his pride, he now said: "Please, Sir, what do you want from me?"

"Now that is better, Mr. Cocksucker. I knew you would start to realize your position. But I hope your mouth does a better job for me than it did for my buddy. Frankly, he was disappointed, thought you would be a better cocksucker than you turned out to be."

Thomas stifled a frustrated sob. "Please, SIR; what do you want?"

"Well, here is what I had in mind. Now that we have gotten things clear between us, we can settle in for a nice quiet evening together here at the hotel. I know you were going to check out tomorrow, but I have extended you for another night. A little later on, we will order room service, but basically, you are going to *be* the room service. Got it, Thomas?"

"Please, I can't extend, I am expected home tomorrow!"

"Oh, that is ok; I talked to Cheryl a little while ago on your Blackberry, told her I was one of your assistants asked to call you with a message. She didn't seem that surprised or concerned. The only other thing now is to contact Mr. Philips. He is your boss, is that right?"

Thomas weakly nodded assent.

"Right, well, I thought you could make that call yourself. I will dial the number for you, and you can talk to him. What you are going to do is read out what is on this little card while I give your faggot balls a nice little massage. You had better do a good job on this, because if you don't, that massage is going to get much less comfortable, understand, faggot?"

Thomas felt a surprisingly strong grip on his cock and balls as the desk clerk expertly pushed a few buttons on his Blackberry and pressed it to his ear.

Alan Philips, probably the most feared partner at Gold Hightower Inc., answered his cell phone on the second ring.

"Please, Sir, this is Thomas," he read from the index card under his nose. I just wanted to say that I can't work late tonight. I am having a nap, as the stress is too much for me."

Thomas hesitated, and a quick pain shot through his balls.

"I hope you understand, Sir, I am just not up to it tonight."

Mr. Philips spluttered as the desk clerk hung up the phone.

"Well, now, that wasn't so hard," said the desk clerk. "Tell you what, just for being such a good little faggot, I will make you a bit more comfortable. How would that be?"

Thomas nodded gratefully, and was most relieved when the bonds were loosened from the chair.

"Strip" came the command, and Thomas hastened to pull off the remnants of his expensive Armani suit, standing now only in his boxer shorts. A stern look from his new Master was enough to make him strip those off as well, and then turn around for handcuffs to be fitted on his wrists behind him.

"Now, Mr. Sutton lets see how you are on boots." Thomas' head was roughly shoved down to the desk clerk's feet, and, amazing even himself, he obediently stuck out his tongue and began to lick the man's rough black Boots.

"Put some passion into it, faggot, or Cheryl gets the videotape in the mail."

Desperately, Thomas increased the intensity of his licking, only pausing momentarily as the Boot was turned up and he was directed to continue on the soles. Tears were starting to roll down his cheeks at the enormity of what he, a rising star at Gold Hightower, was being forced to do. Too late, he saw the flash of a digital camera recording his face and tongue under the Boot.

"Not bad for a beginner, we can work on that later. Now let's see you suck cock again."

Thomas obediently moved up the desk clerk's legs, opened his zipper with his teeth and took a foul smelling half erect penis in his mouth. Again the camera flashed, recording this new indignity. Still, he went up and down on the shaft, surprised to feel his own dick stiffening rapidly between his legs.

"Now fetch". A red rubber ball was tossed across the room, and Thomas crawled over to retrieve it, returning with it in his mouth.

"And again". The process was repeated half a dozen times, with the desk clerk stroking his cock and laughing unashamedly at Thomas' antics.

"All right, then, time for a break." The desk clerk picked up the phone and asked for room service. "One filet mignon, medium rare, with salad and with a bottle of your best red wine, also a second bottle of Dom Perignon. And could you also send up a dog dish and dog food for my puppy? I forget to pack those. Thanks!"

"So, faggot, you can keep sucking on me while we wait, this is your appetizer." The desk clerk stretched out comfortably while Thomas, now terrified, went back to work on his crotch, alternating back to the boots every time the desk clerk snapped his fingers.

Finally, there was a knock at the door. "Better get that, faggot." said the desk clerk, motioning Thomas to turn around so the cuffs could be unlocked. "Here is something to wear; we don't want to be indecent." He tossed Thomas a frilly pair of lace women's panties.

Incredulous, Thomas stared at the panties as the knock at the door was repeated. Slowly, sadistically, the desk clerk made a mock movement with his fingers to signify a camera shutter clicking. Trembling, Thomas pulled the panties over his hard-on and crawled to the door.

Chapter Four

T homas opened the door to see a dignified older waiter carrying a silver tray, laden with his captor's supper, who looked at him incredulously before elbowing past him towards the main room of the suite. As he put the tray down on the table, his eyes swept up and down Thomas' naked body, briefly surveying the pornographic writing and resting on the prominent bulge in the frilly panties. His lip curled in disgust as he dropped the check on the table.

"Looks like I interrupted something," he sneered.

"Help, let me out!" came a male voice from the bathroom, faintly muffled.

"What is going on here?" asked the waiter, snatching up the check.

Thomas stood dumbfounded in his lace panties, the writing still clearly visible on his chest and thighs and the dried cum matting his still neat haircut. About to appeal to this potential savior for his freedom, he now found himself in the position of justifying his admittedly incriminating appearance.

"Look, man, just sign the check; I need to get out of here. I don't like waiting on perverts."

Thomas numbly signed and handed the folder over. The look of disgust given him spoke volumes, before the waiter backed away and hastened to the door, refusing the tip weakly offered to him. Thomas stumbled back across the room, and sat down despondently in the chair. Far from being rescued, he was now ensnared in his predicament deeper than ever.

Slowly, the bathroom door opened, and his tormentor emerged. His Master had taken his shirt off, and was wearing a pair of Thomas suit pants, showing a not very muscular and hairless chest, certainly no match for the physically buffed Thomas. The front of his trousers tented out showing a bulging cock, which he was rubbing meaningfully as he came over and sat down next to the dinner.

"Before we get started, faggot, I had a look through your suitcase and found a few items you can wear to dinner."

Thomas looked up hopefully, and saw a pair of over-the-calf black nylon dress socks dangling from his Masters hand, as well as his still shiny Johnston and Murphy dress shoes in the other. Obediently, he took them and put them on, painfully aware of how ridiculous he looked with this masculine power attire on his feet but nothing else above except the panties and humiliating markings.

Slowly but automatically, he bent down to lay out the dinner for his Master, opening the bottle of Dom Perignon and pouring a portion into the glass, then folding the napkin before offering it up and lifting the metal cover from the hotplate. Then he sat down hopelessly on the floor, hoping against hope that this man would release him after he had enjoyed His meal.

"Go get me some ice for this champagne bucket, faggot!"

Thomas hardly had time to register what had been said before he grabbed the silver bucket and crawled out the door, his heart sinking as he heard the door click shut behind him. Thankfully, no one was in the hall to see him rush to find the ice machine, nor to witness his frantic knocking to be readmitted to the room. When the door was finally opened, he gratefully scurried back in, hardly noticing the glint of his Rolex on the Masters wrist.

"Kneel down, faggot, while I finish my dinner."

The Master ate in silence, but there was a new tension in the room, and soon his foot was extended and Thomas instinctively bent his head to lick it. Surprisingly, he also turned it up so that Thomas could lick the sole. Then he was told to stand up and back, and to put his hands behind his head.

The Master then carefully wiped his mouth with the napkin, took a swig of champagne, then rose, sauntered over to Thomas, and poured the rest of the bottle into his panties. Next came a sharp twisting of his tits, all accompanied by a diabolical smile. When Thomas kneeled again in pain, he saw the Masters Cock tenting out under his pants, and knew that the evening was not yet over. And so he knelt down and licked his boots again in earnest. As he did it, he winced in pain as the Masters foot pressed heavily and painfully into his panty-clad crotch.

Finally, the order came to turn around and put his hands behind his back, and he felt the handcuffs clicking back on. The Master, clearly aroused, now got very aggressive indeed, slapping Thomas around, twisting his tits, punching his balls and biting painfully on his ear. Finally, he was roughly thrown on the bed, and felt the Master putting on a rubber and mounting him from behind. He started to yell in pain when he felt the Cock roughly entering his ass, but the remainder of his expensive silk tie was quickly stuffed in his mouth, and a cruel additional twist made it clear it was pointless to resist. This Master, scrawny and lowlife as he looked, was surprisingly powerful, even without the handcuffs.

As the Cock went in and out, harder and harder, Thomas realized that this truly was rape, very scary, if also a bit thrilling, and a graphic new experience for this arrogant young man used to getting his way. When the Master finally came, He pulled out, threw the used condom on the bed and calmly went to the bathroom to wash up, leaving Thomas cuffed and with his panties still pulled down, lying on the bed.

When he came back, the Master calmly dressed in Thomas other suit, put his things back in his backpack, downed the rest of the champagne, and only then took off the handcuffs and returned them his pocket. "Don't even think about trying to report this" he hissed at Thomas, looking at him with contempt as, incredibly, he turned to go, not answering the confused plea for discretion with the pictures that had been taken. Thomas merely sat there as the door closed, totally humiliated but also relieved that the ordeal was finally ended.

x x x x x

It only took Thomas about twenty minutes to shower, futilely scrubbing the worst of the writings from his body, dress in the filthy jeans and t-shirt left by the Master and pack what was left of his belongings in his Louis Vuitton briefcase. Still very shaken by the experience, but once again feeling a bit like his old self, Thomas shut the door to the room and headed down the hall, this time making a beeline for the stairs rather than the elevator, anxious to make a quick exit without anyone noticing his attire.

"Mr. Sutton, could I have a word with you?" came the voice of a distinguished grey haired man in a suit at the other end of the lobby. Slowly and carefully, he sauntered over and nodded, then followed the gentleman into a small private office adjoining. He felt the man's eyes grazing disparagingly over his dirty and worn clothing.

"Thank you for letting me speak to you in private, I think we both have an interest in solving a rather difficult situation discreetly" he said coolly.

Thomas looked up in incomprehension as the man continued.

"This is a good hotel, and we maintain high moral standards not only for our staff but also for our guests. I as security manager need to enforce those standards. That is why I was really very surprised to receive a complaint from one of our staff, backed up by a witness, of homosexual harassment in your room. Before I file a complaint with the police, and ask you to please leave the hotel, I just wanted to give you a chance to explain and perhaps offer some sort of discreet alternative to compensate this fine young man for what he has suffered. Do you have any suggestions?

Slowly, numbly, Thomas shook his head yes.

NO CHOICE

Written by: Anonymous Cop

I knew better; I knew I was flirting with potential danger, but once again in my life I let my cock overrule my brain. It was mid August, another one of those hot, sunny days when a guy should be at a pool or on the beach and not in a State Police cruiser with the air conditioner barely working. I'd given my usual share of tickets, had lunch and headed for "my spot". That's what I called it…"my spot" because I was sure that no one else knew about it. It was off the main road, down a lane and then further down a small dirt path to a beautiful, small, blue pond with clean cool water. I had found it last summer and had returned this summer on many of the hot days for an hour or two of relaxation.

I pulled up that day, parked the cruiser in the shade under some trees, took out the blanket and towel I kept in the trunk and walked down to the cleared area just before some trees at the pool. In books and movies it seems that the hero always knows when he is being watched, he somehow senses it. Some hero I am. I had no clue. I did look around just in case but didn't see anything out of the ordinary and I believed this place was just too remote for anyone accidentally finding it. I spread the blanket, sat on it and pulled off my boots and socks…oh man that was a relief. You can't imagine how I sweat in those damn boots in the summer. The boots are of top leather quality, made special for each trooper by the department. They are eighteen inches high with another half inch on the heel. They are black and hold a fantastic spit shine, that is, after the initial effort of getting the shine on. After the first effort it just takes a quick buff to keep the shine unless you end up in mud or really scrape them bad. Each trooper is issued two pairs and generally we alternate wearing them. At least I do because my feet tend to sweat heavily, especially in the high white athletic socks I use. I air the boots out every night but still that aroma, which can only be associated with sweaty feet seems to permeate my closet. Next, off came the shirt, the armor vest and my tee. I piled them neatly by the side of the blanket, and then took off my duty belt containing my weapon and other gear. This always bothered me a little but I figured it was just as readily handy there as on my waist and a hell of a lot more comfortable. Next off came the trousers and finally my white briefs. I lay there stretched out totally in the buff, sucking up the rays and deepening my already well defined, full-bodied tan.

And, naturally, very soon my right hand reached down to my cock and started stroking it. Nothing really serious, just slow, gentle strokes which of course eventually led to faster, harder strokes and before I knew it I was hard and horny. I should have stopped right there but hell when it comes to jacking off I just can't stop once I get started. Hey I may be a decorated State Trooper, but I'm a man and I need relief like any other man. And yes, even though I tried my best to delay the sensation I soon erupted in one glorious spasm of cum. Oh God, the satisfaction, the joy, the relief! Most of it landed on my stomach and around my crotch and I knew that I'd have to take a dip in the pond to clean myself off.

But not right away. First enjoy that sun and this feeling of sheer relaxation. But I knew I couldn't stay this way and after a few minutes I got up and strolled down to the pond. I waded in the cool water to a spot that I knew from previous times was deep and clear of rocks and obstacles. I dived down, enjoying the feeling of the water on my sweaty body and swam around for about ten minutes. Reluctantly I pulled myself from the water and headed back through the trees to my gear.

But instead of my blanket, uniform and gear I ran into two guys sitting there watching me. I admit I panicked and looked around for my gear, hoping it was in reach. No such luck. One of them had on tight, dirty jeans, biker boots and a tank top tee that read "Pigs Suck". It was a couple sizes too small so it definitely emphasized his highly developed abs and arms. I'm not really sure how the second guy was dressed because all I could see was the camera in his hands as he took photos of me in my birthday suit dripping wet. I recognized the muscular one as a biker that I had stopped, harassed and ticketed a couple of times.   My first instinct was to grab and smash the camera and apparently I made a gesture, but was stopped by muscles who said, "Relax trooper. Ain't no way you're gonna get that camera. There are two of us and only one of you and let's face it, you ain't dressed for combat."

They both laughed at that and it dawned heavily on me that I was indeed naked. Now I'm not ashamed of my body, quite the contrary, I work out a lot and as I said I had a deep tan, but somehow being naked in the company with fully dressed guys is disconcerting and embarrassing and I felt vulnerable. And taking down the guy with the muscles wouldn't be easy.

"Where is my gear?" I managed to say.

"Oh you mean your uniform, your weapon and all that cop stuff?" It was the muscular one in the tank top who spoke, obviously he was the leader.

"You know damn well what I mean. You better get that stuff back or you are in deep shit you punks."

"No," he countered, "it's you who is in deep shit trooper. How the fuck are you gonna explain to your police bosses the fact that you lost it all? Do you think they will be happy to know that you come out here and j/o while on duty? Maybe they don't now, but they will if we tell them." Again they both laughed.

He was right, how in hell could I explain this away to the brass? It was true I was in deep shit. But I figured I could bluff my way out, or at least try.

"I'll just say you jumped me and then you'll have the entire State Police organization after your asses."

Muscles laughed again. "Something you should know trooper." (And the snide, degrading way he said "trooper" pissed me off even more.) "You see I know about this little secret of yours and I have been watching you for a couple of weeks now. In fact I even have videos of you going through your routine. You think your bosses would enjoy watching them?"

"Bullshit, you don't have any videos. Now give me back my stuff and get out of here and we'll call it even."

"Ah but I do have videos, asshole. Look over there to your right and you'll see one of my buddies with the video camera. He has documented your activities three different times. Great stuff. I figure I can send a copy to your bosses, maybe show it on You Tube, or even combine them and sell them as porno movies. What do you think about that asshole?"

He was right; I checked and a nerdy looking guy stepped out from behind a tree and waved his video camera at our direction. I was truly and absolutely fucked.

"You bastards," was all I could say. "OK how much do you want to give me the videos and my gear?" (Not that I had any great surplus of money that I could use, but somehow I figured I could get it.)

"Oh I don't want your money, at least not right now. What I want asshole, is you."

"Huh? What do you mean? Is this some kind of stupid joke?"

"No joke Trooper," he snarled. "I want you! I want to own you, make you my personal property. And if you don't do what I say then the tapes go to your bosses and all the other places I mentioned."

"You bastard, please don't do this to me."

"Begging won't help, although it sounds good. Either submit to me or the tapes get sent out. It's up to you. Don't sweat it asshole you don't have to make a decision right now. You can think about it for the rest of the day. When your tour is over call me for further instructions. I don't hear from you then the tapes get forwarded. If I do then your secret is safe ….that is as long as you do what I want."

I was stunned. Surely there was some way out of this mess, but what? I needed time to think it out and there was still four more hours left on my tour so maybe I could come up with something. "How do I reach you? I don't know your number."

"Easy asshole. We have your cell phone, took it from your uniform pants. Just call it and I'll answer. I'll expect your call by 6 p.m."

"You bastards," was all that came out of me again.

Muscles looked over at me. "You know asshole you should start learning to treat your superiors with more respect. Try SIR from now on. But don't worry, I'll teach you respect in short order. Now turn around cause I'm gonna hand cuff you."

My wrists were cuffed behind my back and I stood there naked and even more vulnerable than ever. Muscles came over and fondled my balls in his hand. "Nice," he said. Then he felt my ass cheeks. "Nice here too." I blushed; no man had ever done that to me before. I wanted to knee him in his crotch, but I knew that wasn't very smart considering the position I was in. And, I admitted to myself, in a weird way it felt good.

"The key to the cuffs are on the front seat of your cruiser. Your clothes and most of your gear are on the back seat. I say "most of your gear" because along with your cell phone we borrowed your wallet with all your IDs and your badge. So you better call if you want that stuff back or it goes along with the tapes to your boss. Now lay down on your stomach, close your eyes and count slowly to 200, then you can go to your vehicle. Figure that will give us enough time to be well away from here. We wanna go back to our place and watch this latest video. And to make some copies. Should be fun. I'll be waiting for you call."

I did as ordered, heard them laughing as they left and after awhile I heard the sound of motorcycles roaring away. I got up and walked to my cruiser, feeling stupid and panicky. How the hell was I going to get out of this mess? I couldn't give in to them but if I didn't my career was over. I was between the proverbial rock and a hard place. I reached the cruiser and found the key to the cuffs. It took a little maneuvering but eventually I freed myself and got dressed. They were right, my cell phone and wallet were missing. I spent the rest of the afternoon trying to think of what to do. I vacillated between telling them to go to hell and giving in. If I fought them then the tapes would go to the Superintendent's office and I would be out of a job and a reputation. But who knew what would happen if I gave in? I remember muscles saying, "I don't want your money, not yet. I want you."

Fuck man, which could mean anything. My final decision was to play along with him, at least for awhile, to see what he wanted and try to figure out a way to get the tapes. It wasn't going to be easy, but then I had no choice.

I called at six on the dot and whoever answered said, "Is that you dickhead?" I figured it was best to play their game so I answered, "Yes Sir".   He laughed at that and then told me to go to a certain motel on the edge of a nearby town. I was to go to room 69, facing the back of the parking lot and go in. The door would be unlocked. There I would receive my instructions. He hung up before I could ask questions.

I went to my condo, changed into jeans, a polo shirt and loafers and then drove to the motel. I found room 69 easily enough and it was indeed located in the back of the lot away from most other rooms. This motel was one that usually rented by the hour and questions were seldom asked. We had raided it a few times so I knew it well. Usually we were on a drug bust, assisting the local cops, but we all knew of the sexual encounters that occurred there. I panicked a little thinking what would happen tonight if I was with these bastards and a surprise raid was pulled. Fuck, FUCK, no way I could talk myself out of that, especially if some of my trooper buddies were involved. Damn I thought as I tried the door, I'm fucked no matter what the hell I do. Sure enough the door was unlocked and I went into the room and switched on the overhead light. It must have been nothing more than a 50 watt bulb because it didn't do much to light up the place. There was another small lamp on a table by the bed and when I went to turn that on I saw the note, addressed to "Trooper Dickhead"

The instructions were simple. I was to totally strip. In a drawer in a bureau were some cuffs and a black cloth hood. I was to put the hood over my head, cuff my hands behind my back, kneel and then wait. I said "no fucking way" to myself as I had been cuffed and naked once today and that was once too often, but then, once again, I knew I had no choice so I did as ordered. I don't know how long I knelt there, literally in the dark as I couldn't see through the hood, but it seemed like forever.

Finally I heard motorcycles coming to a stop outside, the door opened and I recognized Muscles voice. "Well, well, it looks like the dickhead knows how to follow orders."

With that the hood was pulled off my head and I saw that Muscles, or as I came to know later he was called Bull, was sitting in the only chair in the room. He was wearing tight leather pants tucked into high thick motorcycle boots that stretched out in front of him. His muscular hairy chest was criss-crossed with a thick leather harness. I had to admit to myself that this was indeed one imposing, impressive piece of manhood. The other guy was in jeans covered by black leather chaps with boots and was wearing a black tee shirt. He was no slouch in the muscles department either but compared to Bull was just slightly above ordinary. He had a video camera and was taking photos of me from various angles.

"What the fuck do you want?" I managed to say but before I could get anything else out Bull reached out with his leather gloved hand and slapped me hard across the face. I fell on my side and just lay there.

"Listen and listen good dickhead. You don't speak unless I give you permission. You listen to what I have to tell you. I have these tapes of you jacking off while on duty and if you don't do what I say I will happily send them to your bosses. You know as well as I do that they are reason enough to get you fired, if not laughed out of the State Police. But I don't want that to happen. I like you being a pig. So I'm gonna give you a chance to keep your job if you agree to be my property, my slave so to speak. I'll totally control you and you'll do whatever I say. Disobey or fuck up even once and off go the tapes. And just so you know, copies of the tapes have been given to a couple of trusted friends so if anything should happen to me or Tommy here then the tapes get sent. Do you understand that dickhead?"

"No, I don't" I answered. "What do you mean be your slave? What will I have to do?"

"Whatever the fuck I tell you to do asshole; I will own you; you become my property. You'll wait on me hand and foot; keep my trailer clean; do my laundry; keep my boots and leather in top condition; and most important be my sex slave."

"No fucking way. I'm no queer fag. I don't do sex with a man. No way."

"Ah, dickhead, I know that you aren't a fag…not yet anyhow. But trust me you'll grow to love sucking my cock and rimming my ass and getting fucked up your own ass.

Believe me it is much more erotic than simply jacking off which you seem to enjoy a lot."

"Damn you," I mumbled. "I'm a State Cop. How can I do that? Anyone finds out the result will be the same as you sending off those tapes."

"Dickhead, dickhead, dickhead, don't worry. As long as you behave and obey ALL orders then the secret is safe. On duty you can continue being Mr. Hero cop but off duty you are mine."

I hung my head and I think I sobbed, holding back tears. "I can't, I just can't. Don't do this to me please."

Bull spoke again. "Tommy take the cuffs off dickhead." The cuffs were removed and I lay there on the floor, naked and softly moaning at my predicament.

"Ok, trooper. It's decision time. You can get up and walk out of here and go on your merry way or you can agree to become my property. The choice is yours."

I just lay there for a few more moments, trying my best to figure out what to do. But either way I was fucked. I figured maybe I could play it for a time and see what might turn up that I could take advantage of to get away. And he did say it would be just between us. I had to trust him; I mean what choice did I have? No choice at all!

"Ok," I whispered. "I'll do what you want."

"Ah dickhead, definitely the right decision. But I want it louder and on tape. So kneel again and tell me that you want to be my slave. And make sure you address me as Master, because from now on that's what you will call me."

I knelt back in position, my arms hanging by my side. Tommy was working the camera on me when I said, loud and clear, "MASTER, I want to be your slave."

"Before I accept you as my slave, dickhead, are you willing to totally commit yourself to my service, be totally obedient and ready to do whatever I order no matter what?"

"Yes MASTER. I commit myself totally to your control. I will willingly obey all orders MASTER."

"Good slave. Now what is your name and job dickhead?"

"I am Trooper Daniel Robert Perkins of State Police, Barracks 18, South Division, MASTER, service number 1399."

"That's who you are ONLY when working. Off duty you will be temporarily known as dickhead until I can think of a better name for you. Now since you are off duty, what is your name?"

"MASTER, I am dickhead MASTER."

"Good slave dickhead. Now come here closer and clean my boots with your tongue to show your devotion to your Master."

There probably are more humiliating and debasing things to do in life, but the first time a man is made to kneel and lick the dust, dirt, grime etc off another man's boots is right up there with the worst of them. I couldn't believe how humiliated and stupid I felt as my tongue worked its way into all the crevices and bends of MASTER'S boots. I thought at first I would gag from the taste of leather, shoe polish and oil and I'll never know how I kept it down. But I did and licked those boots from the soles right up the shaft to the tip top and all the while I could sense Tommy filming the entire thing. It was just another tape with which to cement my slavery and submission to MASTER. After awhile I let my mind go blank and just concentrated on the leather of those boots. I would hear MASTER make comments about what a good slave boy I was turning into and that there would be many other pleasures for my tongue as time went on. Then he said, "Good work on the boots dickhead, now since you're up to the top, clean my pants off too."

The pants were more flexible than the heavy leather of the boots but they fitted tightly on MASTER'S legs and my tongue slid easily over them. I could sense the strength and muscles of those legs as my tongue worked to clean the leather.

It was then that I became aware that MASTER had undone the buttons of his fly and his belt and that his cock was hanging outside the pants. And what a cock it was! It was semi-hard at that point and well over 8 thick inches. I guessed it would swell up to over ten and its circumference would rival a Bud Light can. I gasped at the sight of it and pulled my head back away from it.

"Lick it dickhead. Lick that cock head and shaft and watch it grow."

I just stared. "No, I can't." I said. "Please no MASTER."

"I know the first time is tough slave, but you'll get used to it. Now stop acting like you have a choice. Lick it and suck it slave."

I hesitated, staring at the cock. I had never had a man's cock in my mouth before and I had no idea what it would be like. But, as I was discovering about so much of my new life with MASTER I had no choice. My tongue went hesitantly to the cock head and I licked at it. I could still taste the leather from the boots and pants on my tongue, but also a different taste. Not really unpleasant, in fact kind of tangy and meaty. I let my tongue follow the shaft of the cock and soon was licking it up and down and getting amazed at how it seemed to react to my tongue and grow even bigger. I had guessed right about its size and panicked at the thought of trying to get that monster in my mouth. But an order from MASTER, "suck it slave," convinced me to try. I've had some great blowjobs from females I've dated in the past, so I sort of knew what I had to do. I started slow taking just the cock head into my mouth and letting my tongue feel it out; then a little more of the shaft and a little more. I worked slowly taking a little in and then gently pulling out and going back onto it, just a little deeper each time. In and out, slowly; then a little faster. At one point I gagged as the cock banged into the back of my throat, but I got a deep breath and started in again; going faster and deeper.

I felt MASTER'S hands on my head as he started directing and pushing me onto his cock and I felt his ass and crotch muscles begin to work in sync with my sucking. After awhile I began to gasp for breath because this huge man tool was filling my entire mouth and throat, but there was no way I could pull out with MASTER'S hands holding me steady. My brain told me that I was going to die, suffocate to death, but it also told me to keep on sucking and I did. Suddenly I felt the cock stiffen and sensed MASTER tense up and then spurt after spurt of manly cum erupted from the cock and down my throat. I had no choice except to swallow it. I couldn't believe that one man could have that much cum in him, especially as it just kept cumming, each throe of movement seemingly as powerful and filling as the one before it. MASTER kept up his erection for some time after the flow of cum had ceased and the cock stayed in my mouth the entire time. I knew instinctively that it was better not to pull out, even though my jaw was aching from being open so long. Eventually the cock seemed to deflate, but even then it was bigger than mine and most others that I had seen. There was no doubt in my mind that MASTER was one giant of a man, all over.

He pulled his cock out of my mouth and I gasped for air and enjoyed the small pleasure of exercising my jaw to get some feeling back into it. MASTER patted me on the head and said, "Dickhead I think you are a natural cock sucker. But then most cops are. Now use that tongue of yours to clean my cock of any stray cum on it."

Without hesitation I did as ordered and as I was licking the head and shaft clean MASTER asked Tommy if he had taped the scene and Tommy answered that he got every bit from the boot licking to final sucking moments. I shuddered, thinking, still another nail in my coffin; one more tape to keep me firmly tied to MASTER'S will. But what choice did I have? None!

Suddenly one of MASTER'S booted feet was leveled against my chest and I was pushed back onto the floor. I lay there looking up at MASTER who was grinning at me.

"So how did you enjoy your first blow job, dickhead?" I didn't know how to answer and just lay there staring at him. "I asked you a question dickhead and when I ask you something you better answer me, understand?"

"MASTER, yes MASTER. I enjoyed it MASTER," was all I could say.

"Listen dickhead I can see that I have a lot of training to do to turn you into a proper slave. So listen carefully when I tell you something cause I don't like repeating myself. I gave you the privilege of taking in my man juice; that is an honor that I gave you. And when someone gives you something asshole you're supposed to thank them for it. So?"

"Thank you MASTER," I said. "I enjoyed it MASTER."

"Another thing dickhead," he went on. "On duty you can be Trooper Perkins and show your authority to others. But off duty you are nothing but a worthless piece of shit. You aren't a man; you're less than a worm. So no more of using "I" or "Me" or whatever. From now on when you talk to me you refer to yourself as "dickhead" or "slave" or something similar. Understand?"

"MASTER, yes MASTER, dickhead understands MASTER."

"Yeah dickhead I just may make you into a proper slave yet. Now Tommy here has other things he has to do tonight but before he leaves I think you should show him your appreciation for turning you into a movie star." With that both of them started laughing.

'MASTER, yes MASTER'

"Suck him off now slave."

Tommy was lying on the bed, his legs spread apart. I crawled over to him and knelt beside the bed waiting for orders. "Get up here slave and undo my pants. I want to feel that tongue and mouth of yours."

"Yes MASTER," I answered and then screamed as I felt the pain of blow after blow on my bare back. I was stunned and looked up to see MASTER wielding a leather belt. "Listen you dumb shit. I am your Master. You only have one Master and that is me! You are an inferior piece of shit and so naturally all other men are far superior to you. But I am the only one who is your Master. You will address all others as SIR and only me as MASTER."

"MASTER, yes MASTER. Dickhead understands MASTER. Please forgive dickhead's ignorance MASTER."

"OK, this time asshole but do it again and you'll really suffer. Now get to work on Tommy's dick."

I climbed up on the bed, kneeling between SIR Tommy's legs and reached out to undo the snaps and buckles on his leather chaps and the buttons on his jeans.

MASTER, behind me said, "Fuck asshole, no one said you could use your hands. Put them behind your back."

Puzzled, I did as ordered and felt the cuffs being snapped back on. I understood then that I was to use my mouth to undo SIR'S pants. I put my face close to the crotch area and even then could feel the sexual heat coming through the denim. Using my teeth and lips I worked diligently at undoing SIR'S pants, all the time feeling his bulging cock beneath. Eventually I had the pants undone and pulled away enough for that cock to pop out. It wasn't as massive as MASTER BULL'S but it was no slouch either; over 8 inches at least. It was already hard from having my mouth so close to it while I worked to release it from the pants, so there was no need to try to get it up. I was ready to start in sucking when SIR ordered me to lick and work on his balls first. I was a little amazed that his crotch area was completely smooth, no hair at all and it made those low hanging balls seem even bigger. I licked and sucked on them for several minutes listening to SIR moan with pleasure. Finally I felt his hand on my head directing me to his cock and I took it in my mouth. SIR was obviously primed to cum because it didn't take much sucking on my part before I felt him tense up and erupt. Whereas MASTER'S cum had tasted sweet and tangy SIR'S was more sour and thin. And I wondered as I was swallowing it how I could so easily accept the fact that I was eating another man's cum... The thought bothered me but I kept sucking and swallowing.

Finally the cock began to lose its hardness and, having learned from my time with MASTER I cleaned it off with my tongue. I sighed hoping this was the end of the matter but then SIR ordered me off the bed and when I did he pulled his jeans and chaps down to his knees, rolled over on his stomach exposing a solid, muscular, rounded ass.

"OK dickhead," he said. "Get back up here and clean this ass hole out good."

I couldn't believe it. He was actually ordering me to stick my tongue into his shit hole and clean it out. I had heard about rimming an ass but had never seen or done it. I was stunned. I looked over at MASTER, who was filming the episode. Without putting the camera down he ordered, "Do it dickhead, NOW!"

Once again my choices were limited to only one, no choice at all. So I got back on the bed and hesitantly lowered my face to the cheeks of SIR'S ass. "What are you waiting for shithead, do it," he ordered. So I put my cheeks flush up against SIR'S and involuntarily my tongue began to explore a man's asshole. The smell and taste initially were too much and I was sure I'd gag. But I could hear SIR moaning and knew MASTER was watching so I didn't stop. I'd periodically pull out to gasp for air but then would plunge back in. I'm not sure how long this kept up but eventually SIR sighed and pushed me off. I lay on the bed as he got up and pulled his pants and chaps back on.

MASTER said, "What do you say dickhead when someone gives you something?"

I looked over at the two of them standing there. "SIR, dickhead thanks you for letting it service your cock and ass SIR."

For some reason the two of them found this quite funny and began laughing. Dickhead in turn started to sob. I thought now that I had sunk about as far down as any man could sink, but I was wrong. There were even lower depths to which I would plunge.

MASTER came over to the bed; one of his powerful hands grabbed me by one foot and yanked me off the bed. I landed on the floor on my ass stunned at this action. "Listen carefully, dickhead," MASTER said. "Slaves aren't allowed on furniture. They stay on the floor in a kneeling position unless ordered otherwise. Remember that your dumb shit."

Balancing myself as best I could with my wrists still cuffed behind me I managed to kneel. "Thank you MASTER," I said.

I listened while Tommy spoke with MASTER. 'Well, Bull, it's been great but I gotta head out. I'll make extra copies of these latest tapes and send them to the other guys. This one will be the best yet. I think you've got yourself the makings of a fine slave here Bull, but it's gonna need a lot of training."

"Yeah, I agree," MASTER answered. "But it seems to follow orders pretty good so it shouldn't take too much work on my part. But I sure as fuck am gonna enjoy training it."

MASTER then turned to me. "Dickhead, Sir Tommy is leaving. Crawl over here and clean off his boots before he goes."

I did as ordered and was licking the dirt from Sir Tommy's boots when MASTER started talking to me. "You know dickhead," he said, "I knew the first time you stopped and ticketed me that you were slave material. I can spot a submissive cock sucker a mile away and just the way you looked at my leather gave me my first clue. Then the next time you stopped me and made me lean against your cruiser while you patted me down supposedly looking for weapons I knew for sure. The way your hands caressed my pants and around my crotch I knew. I said to myself, shit Bull, here is a pig cop who wants to kneel before you. That's why I had some of the guys follow you and we discovered that pond of yours and caught you jacking off. You've got an impressive body there dickhead and I knew it was meant to serve me. Admit it dickhead you like serving superior men and sucking their cocks and doing what you're told. Tell me this is what you always wanted dickhead."

I stopped licking Sir Tommy's boots and looked up at MASTER. "No, no you're wrong. I'm not like that."

With that Sir Tommy kneed me in the stomach and I fell over. "Don't argue with your MASTER Dickhead. You know he's right; he is always right."

With that Sir Tommy opened the motel room door, said "See ya later BULL. I'll be in touch," and left.

I forced myself back into a kneeling position and looked up at MASTER who had a big grin on his face. "Ah my little cop slave boy – you and I are gonna have a lot of fun together. But first I gotta take a piss. Open your mouth dickhead."

I backed away a bit, staggered at the thought that MASTER was going to piss in my mouth but then once again I realized the only choice I had was to obey, so I opened my mouth wide and closed my eyes waiting for MASTER'S piss.

"Open your eyes dickhead; I want you to see this present I'm giving you." As I did all I saw was a heavy stream of hot, steaming piss coming at me. I worked hard keeping my mouth open to catch and swallow it all, but some splattered on my face and my chest. The warm, salty urine was tangy to taste but I barely noticed that as I was concentrating too hard on just getting it in my mouth. Like MASTER'S supply of cum, his supply of piss seemed never ending. There was no trickle effect, more like a faucet turned on at full blast. Finally it just stopped, as if someone turned off the faucet and MASTER ordered me to lick the final drops from his cock. But just licking it wasn't enough and he forced the entire cock into my mouth once again and with me sucking, it soon ballooned to its gigantic size. I thought that there was no way MASTER could have any cum left in him after what he had used up earlier.

Suddenly MASTER pulled his cock out of my mouth, lifted me up like I was a feather instead of a 190 pound man and tossed me to the side of the bed. He pushed my face down into the bed and kicked my legs apart so that I was leaning over the bed with my ass in the air. I didn't realize what he was doing until I felt the first swift, angry thrust of his massive cock in my ass. The pain was like nothing I had never felt before; it wracked my entire body. I screamed and screamed but with my face buried in the bed's blankets sound didn't carry far. And it began a steady stream of violent thrusts in and out of my ass, each seemingly going deeper than the previous. I couldn't believe the pain, it was almost unbearable and I thought I'd drop dead. But then MASTER'S movements began to slow, they weren't so desperate, so violent. There was a rhythm to his movements and without realizing what I was doing I began to move my ass muscles in sync with his. I don't know how it happened but I stopped my screaming and began moaning. Were they moans of pain or of pleasure, or both? I don't know. And like when I was sucking MASTER'S cock just before he came, I felt his body suddenly go rigid and tense and deep within the cavities of my body I felt the sensation of warm liquid pouring into me. For some reason my brain registered that this probably was similar to lava pouring out of a mountain volcano and inexplicitly I laughed to myself. Or did I cry? I don't know. I don't even remember MASTER pulling out of me, turning me over and ordering me to clean his cum covered cock. I did it without thinking. I even thanked him for fucking me. He laughed and kicked me back down on the floor.

I heard him leave the motel room but I was too beat to try to get up. I just lay there not thinking at all when he came back in carrying a small canvas gym bag.

"That's a nice ass you have there dickhead, but it is gonna need breaking in and widening up if it is gonna take my cock a couple of times a day. No problem, I've got just the thing here for you."

He held out a rubber object which I knew immediately was a large butt plug. Without another word he turned me over and shoved it in my ass. "Yeah that should do wonders for that cunt of yours slave boy."

He picked me up and put me on the only chair in the room, looping my cuffed wrists behind it. Then he took some rope from the bag and tightly tied my chest to the back and my ankles to individual legs of the chair. "I've had a long, hard day dickhead and need some sleep and I don't want you creeping off. Not sure I can trust you yet. But that ought to keep you. Since you paid for this room for two nights…yeah dickhead I used the credit card in your wallet….we might as well get some shut eye here. I don't know if you enjoy bondage as much as you do sex but you better get used to it because tying up slaves gives me a lot of pleasure. Now just a couple more things here in my bag and then we can both settle down for the night."

With that he pulled a black latex hood from the back and worked it over my head covering every part except my mouth and nose. I began sweating from the tight rubber. Then I felt MASTER put something that felt like a rubber ball in my mouth and felt him strapping it tightly in behind. I could breathe but not see or speak.

Master talked to me as I envisioned him taking off his boots and pants and lying on the bed. "Yeah dickhead, you and I are gonna get along just fine. I'm gonna enjoy giving you what you so obviously want. You are mine now dickhead, I own you."

The next sounds I heard were loud snoring. MASTER had fallen asleep.

I was miserable; uncomfortably tied to the chair, both my ass and my mouth sore and stuffed. I thought about what had happened to me this night….I licked boots, sucked cock, drank piss, rimmed ass and got fucked. How low had I sunk? And then I thought about what MASTER had said about me being a naturally born submissive and that this is what I wanted. Could that be true? Of course not, I'm a respected State Police Trooper, this isn't what I want. But then, I wondered, why is my cock hard as steel now and throbbing with a need to cum?

And so began the first day of my life as a slave.

THIS LITTLE PIGGY
Chapter 1. *Nemesis*
Written by: Anonymous Cop

Lt. Harrison, the shift commander, said my biggest problem was that I was too quick to act without thinking through all the consequences first. He was so right as the following events will show. I am where I am now because I acted without thinking and without following either regulations or his advice.

Let me explain, I am a motorcycle patrol officer in a large city on the East Coast. I love my job and the prestige and power that it gives me. On the street I am in command and there are few who argue with me when I stop them for any traffic violation; maybe that's because I'm a fairly imposing individual standing at 6 foot 1 and weighing in at 220 pounds. Of course the tall black leather boots, leather jacket, shiny blue helmet and the Glock-19 on my hip add a lot to the image. I admit I get kind of a happy glow stopping punks and giving them tickets for the maximum fines. In my patrol area I'm well known, and generally the population obeys the speed limits and laws when they know I'm on duty. That is most of them, but there was one rider who flaunted the rules and deliberately taunted me.

There are a number of punk bikers, gays and leather riders in my area and I was proud to say I had cited most of them on one violation or another. This one guy however was tough to catch and became my nemisis. There is this divided roadway in the city which is a great place to catch speeders and I try to reach my quota of tickets on this route. Three or four afternoons a week this black blur on a motorcycle would go by either on the opposite side of the road or while I was off my own bike and unable to give chase. He'd deliberately rev the engine on his Harley as he sped by to piss me off but he timed it perfectly so there wasn't much I could do about chasing or stopping him. If I would lie in wait for him in an alley or behind a truck he just didn't show up. Yet somehow he knew when I was vulnerable and unable to give chase. He became my personal target and I made a promise to myself to make him pay.

It was a late Friday afternoon and I had called in to the precinct to sign out. I was heading home for three long days off and was looking forward to the break. However, I couldn't let this one car get away with going through a red light so I stopped her – a 30 something broad too busy talking on her cell phone to see the light. I enjoy ticketing this type almost as much as some of the punks in the area. Just as I finished writing her up and was heading to my bike, my nemeses sped by and revved his engine. But this time he made a mistake because I was on the right side of the highway and could give chase. By the time I mounted my bike and started after him he was only three blocks ahead of me, and I knew I could catch him.

He twisted and turned down a couple of streets and almost got away from me but when I made the last turn I spotted his Harley heading down an alley and I knew I had him because it was a dead end with no way out. I pulled in and spotted his bike parked near the only door in the building. It's here that I made my first mistake and didn't take Lt. Harrison's advice. I should have called in to the precinct, told them where I was and what I was doing, but I was so determined to get that bastard that I didn't. I dismounted, opened the door carefully and saw that it was a hallway with another door at one end, so I inched up to it and could hear voices on the other side.

And then I made my second mistake. I unhooked the flap on my holster and loosened the Glock inside for more easy retrieval should I need it. I opened the door and stepped into this lighted room and spotted two guys standing off to the side. One, dressed in neck to toe black leather and holding a motorcycle helmet under his arm was my man. I had him now.

"Who owns that Harley outside?" I demanded.

The leather clad rider looked at me and said, "I do, why is something wrong?'

"Yeah, I'm citing you for breaking a number of laws and I'm gonna see to it that it will cost you more than you got."

"You mean you're going take my bike away?" he asked. "Well, ok it that's what you want, here are the keys." And with that he tossed the keys in an arc toward me.

Big mistake number three on my part. I reached up to catch them. What I didn't know was that a third guy was in the room, behind me, and when I reached my arm up to catch the keys he moved in like a ninja and slipped my weapon out of my holster. I let the keys drop as I felt my gun being taken from me and quickly turned to see a Glock-19 pointed at my head.

"Hi pig," the guy said. "My name is Denny and I have your gun. I want you to know that besides being an expert pick pocket, I'm a good shot and unless you do just what we tell you to do, I'm gonna blow your pig head off."

"Listen asshole, that weapon is loaded so stop fucking with it and give it back to me," I said sternly. "You're in deep shit just for taking it and if you don't want to get in any deeper you'll give it back to me now."

Then the leather rider I had chased spoke. "Pig, it looks like you're the one in deep shit. Denny is indeed an expert with a gun and he will put a couple of holes in your head before you can even move. So I recommend you start paying attention and do what we tell you. Killing you is no big deal to us and we can dump your body just about anywhere. No one saw you come in here so no one is going to suspect us. So either do what we tell you or start saying your prayers, piggy."

"Don't call me piggy," I seethed. "My name is Officer Miller to you and I am not going to take any crap from you punks. Now give me my weapon, asshole."

But the punk called Denny didn't even flinch at my speech. Instead he tightened his finger on the trigger and pointed the weapon at my face. Now my helmet is pretty solid material and good for protection against falling off the bike but there is no way it is going to stop a bullet from a Glock-19 at that range. So I decided that for once I better follow the lieutenant's advice and think the situation out. These punks definitely had the upper hand at the moment but I felt that if I played my cards right I could probably reverse matters, so for now it was best to play along and see what they wanted.

"Okay, Okay, put the gun down. I'll listen to what you have to say."

"Piggy, what we have to say is better said with the weapon pointed at you just in case you really don't listen. Now for all of our sakes, why don't you put your hands behind your back and let us cuff you so that we know you're not going to do anything foolish."

"Damn you, I told you that my name isn't Piggy and you better remember what it is because when I get out of here you're going to be hearing it a lot," I spat. But I knew it was foolish to argue so I put my gloved hands behind my back and one of the other guys came around behind me and snapped on a pair of cuffs. I stood there in full uniform, all 6-plus feet of me trying to stare down those punks, but I just didn't pull it off. They had the upper hand and they knew it.

Chapter 2. *Cuffed*

The leather rider, as I thought of him, came up to me. Out of his belt he pulled a sharp looking 6 to 8inch knife and placed it up against my crotch. He said, "Piggy, your gun isn't the only weapon we have. I'm pretty good with this knife and there is nothing I'd like more than cutting your cop balls off and making you eat them." He jabbed the knife gently into my crotch and I could feel its sharp point against my cock. "Now if I was you and I wanted to keep my manhood, I'd do what I'm told. Is that understood?"

"Shit, man listen. This is ridiculous," I said, starting to feel real fear now. "You can't just threaten a cop. Damn you assholes are in so much trouble now that you'll never get out of it. Stop this shit while you can!"

"Ah Piggy, Piggy. Shut the fuck up. We'll tell you when you can talk and what you can say so keep that pig mouth of yours closed until I tell you to open it," the leather biker stated mockingly. "Now, maybe you would like to know who we are and why you're here. In case you didn't notice this is the back room to the BootsNLeather club and you are our guest because you have been harassing and annoying our members and patrons for far too long. Business is falling off because guys don't want to have to fuck with you giving them a ticket for some made-up violations. "My name is John. You've met Denny. That fine looking specimen is Mike. However, from now on you are to address us as either SIR or MASTER. Do you understand?"

"Fuck you!"

Actually they were an imposing trio. John, obviously the leader was just about my size and it was clear that he spent a lot of time in the gym because I could see the firm abs and tight muscles bulging through the leather gear he wore. Mike was smaller, maybe 5'7" or 5'8" and very wiry. He had on jeans with tight black leather chaps over them, black harness boots and was bare chested. Dark black and red tattoos covered his arms. Denny, the one with my weapon, was even more imposing than the others, coming in at over 6 feet of solid muscle. He was a dark skinned black man who seemed to have a perpetual scowl on his face and a manner which said he would be much happier stomping on someone's balls than sipping tea. He had on a tight pair of black latex pants and at first glance it was hard to tell whether he was wearing anything because the pants matched his dark, glistening skin. Only the huge bulge in his crotch gave away the fact that he was in rubber.

John spoke again, "OK, piggy let's go into the next room where we can have a little more privacy and talk in earnest." With that Dennis pushed me from behind and I had no choice but to follow them into an adjoining room. The room was windowless and the walls were covered with black drapes that reached from ceiling to floor. I was marched to the center of the room and told to stand with my feet together. Mike then came to me and removed my helmet and shades. "Well, well, so this is what piggy looks like without his head covering. Not a bad looking dude, a little too much hair but not bad."

I didn't know what he meant by "a little too much hair" since I kept my head in a close cropped military cut. But I didn't say anything, just stood there. Next thing I felt Mike attaching a heavy metal collar around my neck and locking it on. I tried to squirm away from him, but John put his knife to my crotch and said, "Uh uh piggy. Don't fight us dude."

A chain was lowered from a beam in the ceiling and locked on to the collar and then pulled tight. An effective device in that I couldn't move much without the collar choking into my neck.

"Ah, piggy, now that's better, John said. "I believe we can have a nice talk now. Mike why don't you take the cuffs off the officer." The cuffs were removed and my first instinct was to reach up to the collar to see if I could undo it, but that proved futile. "No, no piggy, afraid that collar and chain stays on until we unlock it and as you can tell, there just isn't anything you can do about it," John chuckled. "Now piggy as I told you before, we're pissed at you for all the harassing of our customers that you've done and we think you need to be taught a lesson. Now you just do what we tell you to do and you should be all right; otherwise I'm afraid the consequences won't be nice. Piggy you are now our property, *our slave* and you have to learn to treat us with all the respect that a slave gives to its owners. Do you understand piggy?"

"Fuck you and stop calling me piggy. My name is Officer..........."

"Shut the fuck up asshole. You're name is piggy if that is what we want to call you. And from now on if you speak at all you will call us by our names with MASTER in front of it. Understand piggy?"

I just glared at him and said nothing.

Chapter 3. The Strip

"Now piggy we think that you will better understand if you aren't burdened down with all that gear on, so it might be better to take off your uniform," John said. "What we want you to do is to remove it piece by piece, kind of a pig strip tease. You can start with your duty belt."

What choice did I have? I had to do whatever they wanted until such time as they let their guard down and I could gain control again. So I undid my belt and handed it to the waiting Denny. I was tempted to try and get the pepper spray canister off the belt but I knew that would be useless considering the position I was in.

"See piggy, that wasn't hard at all, was it?" John asked me tauntingly. "Now your gloves and then your jacket."

I took off my gloves, handed them to Denny, then unzipped my leather jacket and handed that to him too. Next on John's orders came my watch, necktie and my uniform shirt. Then my armor vest and tee. I stood there naked from the waist up and vowing to myself that I was going to get even with these bastards if it was the last thing I ever did. They just stood there in front of me, watching, drinking beer and making snide comments.

"Very good piggy," John said, drinking in the sight of my musculature. "Now your regular pants belt and then I guess your boots."

The belt was easy but then I realized that taking off my boots from this standing position and not being able to sit down or even bend over was going to be a problem. I automatically leaned over to work them off my legs but the chain/collar pulled me back and nearly choked me. I didn't know what to do and the men were just sitting there laughing at my efforts, which pissed me off even more. Finally after much stretching, huffing, puffing and sweating I was able to use the toe of one boot to loosen a little of the heel in my other boot. Lifting my knee up as far as it would go I got hold of the bottom of the boot and jerking, twisting, and turning I was able to keep moving it a little at a time.

My captors found this hilarious and laughed and taunted me as I struggled. I had to hop up and down on one leg trying to keep my balance while I worked the boot off the other foot. It took some time but I finally got the left boot off and handed it to Denny who was waiting for it. I was sweating but knew I had to repeat the action for the other boot and went through the same gyrations and struggles until it too finally came off. My captors broke out in loud applause when I finally succeeded.

I stood there panting from the effort, the sweat rolling off me when I was ordered to remove my socks which was only a bit easier than removing the boots. Next came my uniform pants which I was able to unzip and drop to my ankles and then work them off my feet. I stood there in only my jockey shorts and glared at the men.

Chapter 4. **The Shave**

"Great show piggy, great," John said. "You were terrific and I knew you'd do it. Now however we have a few other requests of you. Stretch out your arms so that they are parallel to the floor."

I didn't have it in me to argue so I did as I was told. Mike on one side and Denny on the other quickly fastened metal cuffs to my wrists and then using chains attached them to rings embedded on the walls of the room. They did the same thing to my ankles, pulling my legs apart and chaining them to metal loops embedded on the floor. Soon I was spread eagle and effectively chained to the walls, floor and ceiling and unable to do much more than stand there. John approached me still playing with that knife. He put the edge up against the nipple of my abs and I could feel it almost cutting into me. I flinched but obviously couldn't back away.

"Ah piggy, that's so much better," John mused breathlessly. "I appreciate you much more this way than with all that heavy gear on you. Let's face it piggy, you're pretty vulnerable right now, why I could cut this nip off and there isn't a fuckin' thing you could do about it."

Then he lowered the knife to my crotch and held it against my balls. "Or," he continued, "I could cut your cop balls off and make you eat them. How would you like that piggy, cop balls for dinner?"

I couldn't believe it but feeling that knife pressing up against my balls made my cock grow hard, damned if I knew why.

"Ah piggy, I think you would like that," John taunted me. "Why, just look at the bulge growing in your undies. I think we should get a better look at that what that might be." And with one quick stroke he cut the briefs off my waist. I stood there totally naked with the beginnings of a hard on.

"Hey piggy is getting hard," Mike said. "And damn he's blushing too."

"You bastards," was all I could say and no sooner were the words out of my mouth then I felt this stinging blow on the cheeks of my ass. Denny behind me had whacked me with what I thought was a thick leather strap.

"Piggy," John said, "we don't like to be called names. And you aren't to speak unless you have our permission. Any time you do, you'll be punished. Do you understand, piggy?"

"Fuck You."

With this came a series of blows from behind on my ass and back; one after another, each more painful than the first. But I was not going to give these punks the satisfaction of crying so I held my voice with only a soft groan or moan occasionally escaping unintentionally. After about 20 blows Denny stopped and I stood there ready to fall over but held up by the chains.

"Enough Denny, I think piggy is getting the idea. Just remember piggy you speak only when spoken to and you always answer using MASTER or SIR. Do you understand, piggy?'

I nodded and immediately felt more belts on my rear. 'SIR, yes SIR" I said, wanting to end the beating.

"Ah, very good slave piggy. Mike I think we should do a full body and cavity search of our prisoner to make sure he doesn't have any hidden weapons or worse microphones on him. What do you think?"

"Yeah I agree, but I think we should smooth him out first, just to make sure."

They started laughing among themselves and I didn't understand what they were talking about until Denny stood in front of me with a pair of electric hair clippers in his hands. He started feeling the hair on my chest and I tensed and tried uselessly to back away from him. "Ah piggy," he said, "we're just gonna give you a haircut. Relax."

"No" I shouted, "don't do this!" This of course earned me a couple more whacks with the strap. My body was covered with dark black hair, not overly thick like some bear, but just enough to give it a real viral look. I was proud of that hair and I watched in horror as Denny began cutting it away. I could feel Mike doing the same to my back and when I looked at the floor I could see my hair all around. They used those clippers on almost every part of my body: stomach, chest, back, legs, and arms, even under my arms. I was helpless to do anything but accept it.

After awhile they stopped and John walked around me to examine me. "Well, not bad," he said. "But piggy there still is a lot of stubble and fuzz and I'm sure you don't want that. Mike, get the shaving cream and let's give piggy his money's worth for his hair cut."

And they did, two of them working me over, spraying the lather on my body and then scraping it off with straight razors. I had to stand perfectly still for fear that they might slip and actually cut me. Finally I thought they had finished for good when John said, "Well it's ok, but there is still a lot of hair around piggy's piss tool," and then Denny and Mike began lathering up the hair on my balls and crotch.

"No SIR, please don't," I sobbed.

John answered, "Piggy be good and hold still or Mike might slip and cut off one of those cop balls." They all laughed at this.

Finally there was not one hair on my body from the neck down. John stood in front of me and said, "Piggy, slaves aren't allowed to have hair on their bodies, and let's face it you're a slave. Actually slaves aren't allowed to have any hair at all and I see that we forgot to remove that on your head....a mistake on our part which we will correct now." And they did, shaving off all the hair I had left, even my eyebrows. I just hung my head in shame when they finished and I heard John say, "Piggy you look great...here look at your new self in this mirror." And with that he pulled aside one of the black drapes to reveal a full length mirror and when I looked at the reflection in it I couldn't believe it. I was totally smooth, not a hair on me. I didn't look at all like that tough cycle cop who ruled the area but instead looked like some twink, muscular yes but vulnerable and unmanly. I sobbed at the sight and all of the guys laughed at me.

Chapter 5. Cavity Probe

"Shit piggy, you look great. You'll get used to this we promise." John came to me and began to run his leather-gloved hands over my body. I couldn't believe how soft and cool that leather felt and what a warm, pleasant sensation it was. John started softly rubbing and pinching my nips and I could feel them come alive under his touch. "You like that, Piggy?" he asked me. I answered with a soft moan. John then started gently stoking my cock and as if it had a life of its own it responded by getting larger and harder. The feeling of the leather on my nips and cock was something I had never experienced before and against all of my inner instincts I was enjoying it. I closed my eyes and just drifted into the pleasantness of those hands on my body.

"Ah piggy, I see you like this," John said as he handled me. "Good boy. I wonder if you will enjoy these too." I didn't know what he meant until I opened my eyes to see Mike standing there with a metal pincher device that had two prongs on it, each prong ending with sharp metal teeth, and connected together with a chain. I was a little confused at first then I realized what it was and tried uselessly to back away but Mike was quick and clamped one prong on my left nip and the other on my right. The pain was instant and piercing and despite my best efforts not to, I screamed out.

"What's the matter piggy, can't take a little pain?" Mike teased me. The whole time Mike was attaching the clamps John was playing with my cock and it remained hard. Then he attached a leather device to my balls which effectively separated them and at the same time secured them right under my cock which was now hard and pointed straight out.

"Nice little balls there piggy, but I think they should be stretched to their maximum don't you?" John asked me mockingly. But all I did was moan because the pain in my nips continued to sear through me. That's when Mike came over carrying one of my boots in his hand. He laced a rawhide cord through the loops at the top of the boot and then attached it to the leather cock ring on my balls, letting the boot hang down putting a great deal of pressure on my balls. Now the pain in my balls matched the pain in my nips and I was moaning and groaning in misery.

Denny was next to add to my torture by attaching small but heavy weights to the chain separating the clamps on my nips. Each weight pulled the nips harder intensifying the pain. I was in total agony.

John stood back and looked at me and smiled, "Ah piggy does it hurt you little baby?" I was in too much pain to bother getting upset at the jibes. "Now," John continued, "I think you are ready for that cavity search we need to take.'

Denny came in front of me pulling on a pair of latex gloves and making a big show of snapping them in front of my face. "Oh no," I moaned, "don't do that, please."

John kicked at the boot dangling from my balls and pulled the chain on the clamp on my tits and the combined pain seared through me and a scream escaped my lips. "Piggy, piggy, piggy," he said, "what did I tell you about calling us Sir or Master when you speak to us?"

"Sir please SIRS PLEASE, don't do this to me"

"But piggy we have to," John insisted. "We have to be sure that you don't have a microphone hidden on you and are broadcasting this back to your fellow cops."

"No, no SIR, honest, I don't. PLEASE SIR......" but it was too late because at this point I felt the cheeks of my ass being pulled apart and felt a rubbered finger probing into my anal cavity. At first it wasn't any worse than the doctor's probing at my annual physical but then one finger became two and three and the pain seared through me. I screamed and pleaded but Denny kept probing and digging and I kept screaming.

Chapter 6. *The Bench*

I realized that these punks were slowly breaking me down and I resolved to myself that I wouldn't give in. I'd fight them. I knew I could take whatever torture they handed me and I wasn't going to give in to them. I just had to brace myself mentally for a little pain and humiliation. Little did I know what they still had in store for me.

"I think piggy is getting tired and his muscles are beginning to strain being in this spread eagle position for so long. What do you think gentlemen? And how about you piggy, would you like to change positions for a rest?"

"SIR, yes SIR, please…." I mumbled.

Denny and Mike undid the chains holding my arms and the one on my neck. You can't believe the relief I felt in letting my arms fall to my sides. I fleetingly thought about fighting them, but was too beat to do it and besides my ankles were still chained spread eagle to the floor. The boot was removed from hanging on my balls but the clamps remained on my nips. My balls ached but not as badly as when the boot was attached and my nips were numb beyond any stinging pain. My ankles were then released and with two of the guys holding me up I was dragged over to the side of the room where there was a bench like device set up.

It was just a bit lower than waist high with a circular pattern cut out on one side and an attached platform for my knees to rest just before it. John had me kneel on the platform and my stomach fit nicely into that circular space. The top of the table was padded with foam rubber and with help from Denny and Mike I lay my chest on it. It felt so damn comfortable after having my limbs stretched for so long that I sighed contently and even said, "SIRS thank you SIRS." I mentally kicked myself for that because I had forgotten my resolve to fight these punks and not give into them. Having no pressure on my arms or legs was such a relief that I closed my eyes in contentment. However, I should have been paying more attention because the next thing I knew my wrists had been fastened to the sides of the table and my legs strapped to the stool and although I was in a different position, kneeling instead of standing spread eagle, I was as helplessly bound as before. But for the most part it felt good to have the pressure taken off my arms and neck from having been stretched out taut. The most uncomfortable part of the position was the fact that my head hung over the edge of the table and this became even more uncomfortable when John used leather straps around my neck to keep my head firmly in place. I could move it slightly from side to side and up and down but it was impossible to move it up any distance.

Chapter 7. *My First Cock*

It was then when I felt my ass cheeks being spread apart and heard Mike and Denny talking, although I didn't know which man said what. All I heard was, "Damn, what a nice tight ass that is." "I can't wait to slip my dick into that." "Think we should lube it up first or go in dry?" "I've never fucked a cop before, piggy will be my first." And I realized what they had planned.

"NO, NO SIR, PLEASE, don't fuck me. PLEASE SIRS. Don't use me like a woman. PLEASE. I'm not a fag. PLEASE DON'T DO THIS TO ME SIRS."

I think I was sobbing when John stood in front of me. He said, "Piggy, piggy quiet. You know you don't have any say in this. You're our slave and slaves exist only to please their MASTERS. And if it pleases us to fuck you, then you should be happy about that."

"PLEASE MASTER JOHN," I sobbed. "Don't do this to me. I'll do anything you want, only please don't fuck me. PLEASE."

"Hmmm," John murmured. "Well, piggy we usually don't concede to a slave's desires, after all slaves have no say in anything. But since you're so new to this, we'll try to understand. I'll talk it over with the boys and let you know what we decide."

The three of them went behind me and I could hear them whispering and occasionally laughing. Then John came back and faced me.

"Piggy," he said. "The thing is we're all pretty horny and hard right now. I mean seeing that smooth cop body of yours all ready for us is pretty tempting, if not down right enticing. But we're not totally sadistic uncaring MASTERS so we decided to give you a choice."

I was so relieved that I couldn't stop myself, "Oh MASTERS, SIRS, thank you SIRS."

"I said a choice piggy," John continued. "We need to get off one way or another. So if you'll just give each of us a blow job we might consider skipping the ass raping."

"Blow you?" I asked incredulously. "Oh no, no, I can't do that. I've never had a cock in my mouth. No, no please. I can't..."

"Well, piggy that's your choice," John said. "Either you suck us off or we go in through your ass. Which is it?"

What could I do? I knew they were serious and that if I didn't suck their cocks then I would be raped up the ass. So, reluctantly, I said, "Ok, I'll suck your cocks."

"Piggy, that didn't sound too enthusiastic," John stated. "We want you to be pleased with this honor. You are going to ask me nicely, beg me even, and show me how much you really want my cock in your mouth. Unless I think you are really sincere about this, then it just isn't worth it and I'll have to fuck you instead."

So I said it, "MASTER JOHN please let me suck your cock."

"That didn't sound any too enthusiastic and happy to me piggy. You can do better than that."

"MASTER JOHN SIR, please SIR, piggy would be honored if you would let me suck your cock SIR. PLEASE SIR I'm begging you for this honor SIR," I drawled.

"Ah piggy, that is much better," Jon said happily. "I'd be happy to let you suck me off, but I want to know if you are planning to swallow my cum like a good little slave boy."

"MASTER JOHN SIR, piggy will be happy to swallow all your cum SIR," I said, not believing myself the words that were coming out of my mouth.

"Good slave boy, piggy," John said. He stood in front of me and my head. My mouth was exactly level with his crotch. He slowly undid the belt from his pants and then unzipped them. He loosened them a little and then let the leather pants slip down around his knees. When the pants fell I saw that he was wearing a black jock and I couldn't help but notice how large the bulge was protruding under it. I panicked a little at the thought that a huge man-cock was waiting for me under that jock. John put one of his leather covered hands on my shiny head, rubbing it gently. "Piggy," he said, I know this is your first time and I want to make sure you enjoy it too. Have any of your girl friends ever blown you piggy?"

"Yes SIR," I answered.

"Ah, then you know what has to be done. I won't rush into this, piggy; I'll go nice and easy for you this time. Start out piggy by kissing my crotch through the jock."

What could I do? The cock filled jock was right in my face so I tentatively moved my lips closer and kissed it. I could feel the cock inside jump a little when I did this and I tried to back away, but of course with my head strapped in like that I couldn't. John's jock smelled musty and pissy.

John's leather hand continued to stroke my bald head, occasionally playing gently with my ear lobe and I don't know why but for some reason this excited me and I could feel my own cock getting harder.

"Now piggy I'm going to drop my jock and I want you to kiss my cock head. Do you understand piggy?"

I think the hand playing with my head and ear sort of hypnotized me, because I answered without pause, "Yes SIR"

John pulled down the jock and I was looking at this semi-flaccid cock of about 6 inches. I could only wonder how large it would be when fully hard. I didn't hesitate; I reached out and kissed the cock head. I was surprised that this didn't repulse me but it didn't. I kissed it again.

"Good slave, piggy. Now I want you to use your tongue and lick that head…lick it all over and then lick up and down my shaft."

In my head I said, "Yes Sir," but no words came out of me because I was doing exactly what John had ordered. I licked the cock head and then began going up and down the shaft which seemed to grow bigger and harder the more my tongue worked. I was aware of a musky aroma coming from the crotch and somehow found it intoxicating. John kept rubbing my head and my ears and whispering gently to me. Before I knew exactly what I was doing I had his cock head in my mouth. Then a little bit more of the cock itself, now grown to a hard 9-plus inches. In my head I was amazed that sucking on this cock didn't bother me and once again I wasn't repulsed by what I was doing. I know that John was working with me but somehow I was unaware of how much as more and more of the cock found its way into my mouth and down my throat. At one point I gagged a little but John soothed me and soon I was back at the job of swallowing that cock. Then John's movements began to pick up, the cock was coming in and going out of my mouth, slowly at first and then faster and faster. I worked hard on sucking that cock, conscious only of that man tool in my throat. I could feel the cock throb and beat inside my mouth and feel it bang against the back of my throat. And somehow I could feel John's excitement and when he tensed up and moaned I knew that I had succeeded. It seemed like spurt after spurt of sticky sweet cum erupted from his cock and since it had no other place to go I had to swallow it. But again no repulsion. It wasn't a taste I was used to, but it wasn't one that bothered me either.

John stayed inside my mouth/throat for several more moments until his cock settled back down to its normal size and then he pulled it out. "Ah piggy," he said, "for a first time you did an excellent job. You still have much to learn, but I think you just may be a natural-born cock sucker. And I can see that you actually enjoyed that too." With that he took my own cock in his leather covered hands and gently massaged it. I was ready to explode but he stopped before I could, "No piggy, you haven't earned the right to cum yet."

I don't understand why but I said, "Thank you MASTER John" to him.

Chapter 8. Mike's Turn

John stepped back and Mike was in front of me and I could see the huge bulge in his jeans. "Well piggy?" he asked and once again I begged a man for the honor and privilege of sucking his cock. I was mortified and humiliated but I knew I had no choice so I begged. Mike quickly agreed and soon undid his fly and pulled the jeans back over his leather chaps. He wasn't wearing a jock or even briefs and when the pants dropped his cock sprung out. It looked bigger than John's but I think that was because it was thicker...almost twice as thick, with huge hairy balls hanging below it. I hesitated; positive that there was no way I could get that cock into my mouth and throat. Mike put his hands on my head and directed me to his cock. "Lick it shit head, lick it all over," he said. And I did; first my tongue licking the cock head and slowly, gently taking the shaft into my mouth. However Mike wasn't interested in a slow, gentle suck and he started vigorously fucking my face, moaning, shouting, almost singing as he rammed that huge cock back and forth into my throat. I tried but just sucking was impossible; I couldn't adjust to his thrusts and rams. My throat began to ache and hurt and it was difficult to just stay open for him. I felt that huge cock banging against the back of my throat. Once again I became aware of the musky, intoxicating aroma from Mike's crotch, this time mixed with the smell of leather. It was a heady smell and I quickly thought how much I enjoyed it but this thought was soon gone as Mike increased the tempo of his thrusts. I could feel his huge hairy balls banging against my chin and cheeks. I honestly tried to work with him but it was useless. Fortunately he came quickly – first the taste of pre-cum on my tongue and then huge sticky spurts of cum pouring out of his cock and into my throat. Mike didn't wait for his cock to go down before taking it out of my mouth; instead he pulled it out, cum still dripping from it and wiped it on my cheeks and forehead.

He stood in front of me, zipping up his pants and smiling broadly. "Well piggy, did you enjoy sucking my cock?"

"Yes SIR, thank you SIR," I murmured.

Chapter 9. *Denny*

That left only Denny. My throat was sore and raw and I would have given anything for a glass of water. However no water was given to me so once again I found myself begging a man for the honor of sucking his cock. Denny came in front of me, the snarl still on his face and the bulge in his rubber pants bigger than even before. I had pretty much resigned myself to my task at this point and started in on my plea to let me suck his cock. He stood there in front of me, his hands on his hips, glaring at me. I had to admit to myself that the man frightened me; he seemed to possess absolutely no sign of gentleness or kindness in him. He was an animal and I could feel the monster heat and drive oozing out of him. Out of nowhere his right hand slashed against my face and had I not been strapped in it would have knocked me to the floor. I was stunned and looked at him amazed. I couldn't stop myself and shouted, "You bastard, you asshole. Why did you do that?"

Denny just laughed a low evil sounding laugh without any amusement in it. "You fucking pig, "he said. "I hate the sight of you. Pig cops have caused me nuttin' but trouble all my life and I hate all you assholes. I lost my license to ride my bike because of a ticket you gave me shit head and I plan to get even for that. Don't worry you'll have lots of chances to eat my black man cum which tastes much better than a honkie's, but

I've waited a long time for that ass and I'm going to take it now. So get ready piggy boy cause I'm about to pop your virgin cop cherry."

"No," I screamed. "You promised you wouldn't if I sucked your cocks. I'll suck it only don't fuck me, PLEASE."

With that he slapped me again, "shut up shit head. I didn't promise anything and you don't have a fuckin' say in this. I want that ass and I'm going to take it."

I hollered some more, screamed, called them all every name I could think of. I tried struggling to get free but of course that was impossible. I heard one of the others say,

"We're gonna need that ass later Denny so maybe its better you don't tear it apart right off. Use some grease, don't go in dry."

I was still cursing and swearing at them as I felt my cheeks separated and a cool, damp substance shoved up, in and around the crack in my ass. I watched in the mirror in front on me as Denny pulled down his tight black latex pants then a black latex jock and I saw the biggest, thickest cock I had ever laid eyes on. And since it was black it seemed twice as menacing. I begged some more, swore, cursed and struggled. Mike came around and before I realized what he had done, inserted a rubber ball gag into my mouth and fastened it tightly in back of my head. My pleas and curses were now nothing more than mumbled groans. John approached and told me to quiet down. "Relax piggy. Don't fight this. There is nothing you can do to stop it, so enjoy it. Once you get used to it you'll love the feeling. Do like you did with when sucking our cocks, work with Denny, and don't fight him."

I called John some names and screamed out curses but of course all that was heard was unintelligible mumbles and groans. And then I felt it. My ass was being penetrated, not as before by a couple of fingers but by a man's cock...a huge black cock. There was nothing gentle about Denny's initial thrust...he jammed into my ass and it seemed to go through my entire body. The pain that ripped through me was intense and I screamed into the rubber gag. And as fast as he had gone in me, he pulled out, and just as quickly thrust back into me before I had a chance to resist or relax. Denny kept this up....thrusting in and out of my ass until he slowly stopped pulling out all the way and began a steady rhythm of just hard quick pumping inside me. Somehow the pain subsided a little and as he worked a steady rhythm I began to feel a warm fulfilling sensation inside me. "No," I thought to myself, "I can't be enjoying this. I'm being raped. This is horrible."

I can't tell you how long Denny kept it up, all I remember is that it seemed like an amazingly long time and I was praying for it to end. The pain was no longer strong and intense but the horror and humiliation remained. Then I felt Denny tense up, felt his cock erupting inside me, felt him exploding, and heard him moaning. But I didn't feel anything inside me. I thought I'd feel his cum seeping into my ass the way I had felt the cum from the other guys in my throat. But no, nothing.

Denny pulled out as abruptly as he had first entered me. I could feel the ache and strain on my ass and I sighed knowing he was through. He came around in front of me and at the same time John removed the gag from my mouth. I wanted to swear some more at them but I just couldn't work up the energy. John was rubbing my head again (and damn it felt good) and talking gently to me. "See piggy. I told you that you would enjoy that. Look how hard your own cock is now. Getting fucked really turns you on." Of course I couldn't see my cock but I could feel it and I knew he was right about it being hard. I was even more embarrassed and humiliated.

Denny stood directly in front of me and when John told me to open my mouth, I did it without thinking. And that's when Denny began dumping a cum-filled condom into my mouth. I tried to lock my lips shut but it was too late, most of the cum was in my mouth and throat and the remainder dripped on my chin. I swallowed what I could because I instinctively knew better than to spit it out at them. Denny just laughed at me, "See piggy I told you that you'd taste real honest black man juice before long. Did you enjoy it shit head?"

I don't know why but I was the maddest then that I had been since this whole horrible torture session had begun. I lashed out at him, calling him a black bastard, an asshole, a prick and I included the rest of them in my tirade. They all just laughed at me as I spewed my frustrations.

John said, "Well piggy, that's not the way to address your masters. I think you need to be punished for that. You have to learn to be a better slave piggy."

Chapter 10. *A Soothing Salve*

I was untied from the table and brought back to the center of the room. My hands were cuffed together and pulled up to the ceiling hook by a chain and my feet were fastened again spread eagle to the metal rings on the floor. John then attached my boot back on to the cock ring and the weight of it dangling beneath me increased the pain. Mike came over and pulled a hooded rubber gas mask over my head and face. I could breathe through it with no problem but it was tight and uncomfortable on me. John said, "Piggy it's time that we went out and checked on how the club is doing so we are going to have to leave you alone here for awhile. The gas mask is in case you start to holler. No one is likely to hear you, but feel free to yell as much as you want. And oh we haven't forgotten all those names you called us back then so of course you will have to be punished for that. And I don't think you are going to like the punishment."

With that he showed me a 6 inch dildo covered with a white salve. "This should keep you occupied and thinking of us while we do our job," John said. "We want you to try and concentrate on ways you can best serve us and please us and make yourself into the best slave possible."

While John was talking Mike had come over and was rubbing my sore balls and cock with a white salve. At first it felt cool and comforting but quickly the coolness left and my balls began to feel like they were on fire. I started to jerk around, hoping to stop the pain and heat on my balls and before I knew what was happening Denny had shoved the dildo up my still sore ass. Soon both my crotch and my ass were on fire and I was screaming into the gas mask. I realized that the salve was Ben Gay and it was killing me.

John smiled at me and said, "Piggy the more you jerk around the more you're gonna hurt. If I were you I'd just try to relax. Just in case we'll cover up that asshole of yours with some duct tape so the dildo doesn't fall out when you jerk around. We'll be back in an hour or so and the Ben gay should be worn off by then. Have fun piggy."

Mike passed by and said, "Don't go away piggy, there is more to come." All three of them left me tied there screaming into the gas mask, jerking and jumping in an effort to take the pain away. But of course there was nothing I could do but accept my fate. My body continued jerking and struggling – anything to relieve the pain and stinging fire of the Ben gay. Nothing eased it. The more I struggled the more it burned. My jerking motions would start the boot tied to my balls swinging and the weights attached to the chain on the tit clamps to pull down harder. The more I moved the more pain I was in. Eventually, I stopped screaming but I could feel myself crying real tears inside that rubber mask. I was miserable, more in pain than I had ever been in my life. Somehow my brain separated itself from the pains of my body and I began to think. I thought of what these punks had done to me....stripped me, shaved me, laughed at me, taunted me, beat me, used me for their sexual pleasure even fucked me. It took awhile but eventually I accepted the fact that yes they had defeated me; they had beaten me down; they had destroyed my will to resist. I was their slave and I would do anything they wanted for now. All I wanted was for the pain to stop. But once I was free then I would get my revenge.

I'm not sure how long they were gone but by the time they returned most of the intense fire from the Ben gay had subsided and I had stopped struggling in my bonds. I just hung there by my wrists, my body aching, my face covered with sweat inside the gas mask, a beaten man. Mike was in front of me, standing there with the tube of Ben Gay and saying, "Looks like the first layer has worn off guys. We better put some more on to help ease this shit head's aching muscles."

"No, no, please no more SIRS," I shouted into the gas mask. Mike said, "What did you say, piggy. I can't hear you, speak up asshole."

I shouted louder, "NO MORE SIRS....MASTERS...PLEASE...PIGGY WILL BE YOUR SLAVE. I'LL DO ANYTHING YOU WANT...ONLY PLEASE NO MORE."

Chapter 11. The Twins

My face was dripping with sweat inside the gas mask but I still screamed louder to them not to apply more Ben gay. Denny came to me and began jerking the weights attached to the chain on the nipple clamps while at the same time kicking the boot tied to my balls so that it began to swing back and forth. The pain from both these areas tore through me and I screamed even louder. "MASTERS, I'LL DO ANYTHING, ANYTHING YOU WANT, ONLY PLEASE NO MORE...PLEASE."

John approached and said, "Piggy are you saying that you want to become our slave and serve us as we see fit?"

'YES MASTER," I screamed into the mask,   "I'LL DO ANYTHING YOU WANT. PLEASE LET ME SERVE YOU, PLEASE MASTER."

"Ah piggy, that is so nice of you, wanting to serve us. And I do think you mean it too. I think you are really sincere about this. Denny go relieve the Twins while I release piggy from his bonds."

The gas mask was taken off and what a relief it was to breathe the fresh air again.

I took deep gulping breaths. Next the boot was removed from my nuts and the tit clamps taken off. The worst pain of all was as the blood surged back into the nerve ends where the clamps had been. I screamed, moaned, yelled, and cried all in an effort to reduce the stinging pain but to no avail. They let me hang there until the pain subsided a bit and then John undid the cuffs and my arms fell uselessly to my sides. Next he removed the chains from around my ankles. For the first time in hours I was not shackled to anything. I fell to my hands and knees on the floor. John stood above me, his hands on his hips looking down at me. I said, "Thank you Master." I didn't look up at him, but kept my eyes on the floor. He walked closer to me and soon his boots were directly under my gaze.

"I think you should show your appreciation for this privilege, Piggy," he said.

Without looking up I responded, "Yes MASTER, thank you SIR." With his boots right there in front of me I realized what he wanted and immediately began licking them, from the toe to the heel and up the shaft, cleaning them, making them glisten with my tongue.

"Good boy piggy. You've earned a reward; how would you like some water?"

I realized then how parched I was and answered, "MASTER, yes please SIR that would be great." I was thinking they would give me a glass of water but instead Mike put a bowl in front of me and I knew instinctively that I was to lap it up the way a dog does. I was too beat and thirsty to argue or feel embarrassed so I set to work immediately lapping the water with my tongue. Amazingly it wasn't that difficult and I soon had finished the bowl, although some water had spilled on the floor.

"Ah piggy, you did that very well. You'll make a fine puppy dog and we'll give you all your meals that way. Would you like that?"

"MASTER, yes SIR. Thank you MASTER."

Then I heard the door open and the sound of boots on the floor, but I didn't dare look up to see who it was. John said to me, "Piggy you claim that you will do anything we ask now that you accept the fact that you are our slave. Well our hard working bartenders are here and they need a little relief from all the work they've been doing. I think it would be fitting for you to have sex with them. Would you like that piggy?"

"Yes MASTER, that would please me very much SIR."

Still on my hands and knees and not daring to look up I was led to the bench where I had previously been tied. John told me to get into the same position but this time they didn't bother strapping me in. It was then that I had my first look at the twins. Two men built almost exactly alike, both in tight leather pants and knee high spit shined boots. Identical leather harnesses crisscrossed their massive chests, and massive they were. Leather hoods with eye holes covered the top half of their heads. Leather arm bands emphasized the bulging muscles of their powerful arms. These were undoubtedly two of the most impressive male bodies I had ever seen and in spite of myself I gasped.

"Ah piggy," John said, "I see that the twins appeal to you. Good, because you will be seeing a lot of them in the future. Now gentlemen, since piggy has so willingly agreed to have sex with you, which one of you wants to go first?"

One of them spoke. "Shit this fucker has two holes doesn't he? We'll fill them both at the same time. As long as we get off what difference does it make? The fucker doesn't have any diseases does he?"

"Do you piggy?" John asked.

"SIR no SIR, piggy is healthy SIR."

With that one of the twins walked behind me and I could sense him studying my ass and heard him say, "Hmmmmm, not bad." The other came in front of the bench and without a word dropped his leather pants and moved in close to me. His cock was in perfect proportion to the rest of that big muscular body and it swung out already hard and swollen. I didn't hesitate but instead leaned into it and started to tongue the cock head.

To my surprise he slapped my face hard and I amazed myself by not moving or complaining. "I like my balls worshipped before you get to my cock fucker. So lick 'em, suck 'em, worship them shit head." I wasn't quite sure how to go about this but I figured the best bet was to begin by licking them all over. Like my newly shaved crotch, his was perfectly smooth. I started licking those balls and soon had one of them inside my mouth rolling it around and gently sucking on it. Strangely I thoroughly enjoyed the taste of those huge balls. I don't know how long I worked on the balls, first one then the other – they were too big to try to get them both into my mouth at the same time. I was concentrating my whole being into worshipping them and then slowly began on the cock itself. Licking, kissing, and pleasuring it. First the head and then slowly the entire shaft was taken into my throat. Not an easy job because this was the biggest cock I had ever seen. I now knew what was meant by a cock the size of a beer can. My jaws, throat and neck ached but somehow, for some unknown reason, it wasn't painful. I was turned on by sucking that cock.

I realized at one point that the twin in back of me had been massaging the cheeks of my ass and I was enjoying the sensation. I felt him pull them apart and became aware that he was entering me. I had a momentary panic when I wondered if his cock was the same beer can size as the one in my mouth and thought that if this was the case then without a doubt he would tear my ass in two. No way could any man take that.

I didn't get to actually see that cock but I could tell it was huge. Yes there was pain as it penetrated deeper and deeper, but he used his cock in a different way from Denny's out and out rape. His penetration was gentler, more sensual. The pain mostly disappeared and soon I was filled with a deep warmth and satisfaction.

The twins must have done this before because I became aware that the rhythm of their movements were in perfect sync and that it didn't take my body long to adjust to this rhythm. I was stunned because I knew I was enjoying this sensation. Then it happened, practically in unison they tensed up. Both cried out, almost exactly at the same time and both shot their loads into me. I wish I could better explain the feeling of someone erupting into your ass at the exact moment someone else erupts into your mouth. Absolutely amazing! Sensational! Fulfilling! Exhilarating! I didn't realize how much I was turned on by it all until I felt the tensing up of my own cock and experienced the sensation of bursts of cum pouring out of it. I was vaguely aware of my three MASTERS laughing but I was too excited to care.

The twins pulled out of me, again in unison I'm sure, the one in the rear coming to the front with his buddy. "Not bad fucker. Yeah, you just might do." And with that they zipped up their leather pants and left.

Chapter 12. The Polygraph

I continued kneeling on the bench waiting for my next orders. I was beat and would have given anything for a bed to lie down and sleep. But of course that wasn't to be. John ordered me off the bench and told me to kneel before him. I did, keeping my head down looking at the floor at all times. John was speaking to me. "Piggy lots of scum like you have said they wanted to be our slave but time and again we learned that many of them were lying. They didn't want to be a true slave; they just wanted some sexual enjoyment. How do I know which you are piggy? Do you really want to be our slave or are you just lying to get a little cock?"

"MASTER piggy wants to be your slave SIR. Piggy wants to serve my MASTERS."

"Ah piggy, you say that but how can we be sure its true. Would you be willing to take a lie detector test to let us know if you are telling the truth?"

I had no idea what he was leading up to but I gladly agreed to take any test they wanted. With that they led me, crawling on my hands and knees, into still another room where a large wooden chair was positioned in the center. I was told to sit in the chair and I hesitated when I saw a 4 inch dildo fastened to the seat. John said, "Sit on the dildo piggy; we want you to be centered and secured snugly on the chair." As with this whole horrible ordeal I had no choice and eased my sore ass slowly down on the rubber dildo as best I could without additional pain. However after having the cocks of Denny and one of the Twins, this dildo offered no pain at all. Leather straps were used to fasten my arms to the arms of the chair and other straps were tightened around my chest and fastened to the back of the chair. My feet were secured in a like manner to the legs. I was strapped in like the electric chair and I panicked a little. I panicked more when Mike began attaching small electrodes to my nips, fingers, toes, and even my once again erect cock. Wires came out of the electrodes and ran behind me. Finally a metal band was placed on my head and tightened down over my forehead. It too had wires attached. I had no idea what was happening but I began to sweat with fear.

"Ah piggy, don't worry. We are not going to electrocute you. The wires are attached to the lie detector machine which Denny is operating. What will happen is that we will ask you a question and if you tell a lie the machine will record it. Surely you've seen polygraphs in your work before."

"Yes SIR," I responded; only I knew I had never seen one quite like this one.

"OK piggy, we're all set. We have a series of questions to ask you and we want you to answer them all with total honesty. Is that understood?'

"SIR yes SIR"

"Oh and piggy, make sure you answer them with respect the way you've been taught."

"SIR yes SIR"

"OK, we'll start out easy. What is your name?"

Without thinking I answered, "Officer...," and that is as far as I got because jolts of electricity went through me in all parts of my body: my ass, my cock, my nips, my head. If I hadn't been strapped down to the chair I'm sure I'd have jumped to the ceiling.

"Piggy, Piggy, Piggy. What are we going to do with you? Now you know your name, so answer correctly. Now once again what is your name?"

Although I was still stunned from the jolts of electricity, I knew what the answer was and said, "Piggy."

Zap…another jolt of electricity ran through me. I screamed out, tears running down my face.

"Piggy, I told you to answer questions with total respect for your Masters. Now for the last time, what is your name?

"MASTER, I am piggy MASTER."

No surge of electricity. "See piggy how much easier it is to tell the truth. One other thing which isn't your fault because we haven't taught you everything yet. But slaves aren't allowed to use the first person singular. Ever. You never refer to yourself as 'me' or 'I' or even 'he'. Piggy a slave is the lowest form of life. You are an 'it'. You can refer to yourself as 'it' or as 'this asshole slave' or 'this stupid shit' or some such aptly descriptive phrase, but never 'I 'or 'me'. Understood? So please one more time, what is your name?"

"MASTER, it is called piggy MASTER."

"Very good piggy, now you're learning. Ok let's get on with the test. Your next question is, "What is your job?"

"MASTER it is a police officer MASTER."

ZAP…the electricity tore through me. I screamed even louder this time.

"Piggy, piggy, piggy. Think before you tell those lies. Now think and the tell me what your job is"

"MASTER, piggy is a slave MASTER."

"So true piggy, so true. "

"Next question, what are your duties, piggy."

"MASTER, piggy's duties are to serve its MASTERS.

And so the test went on. There were a series of questions and whenever I didn't give the answer MASTER JOHN wanted, I got a jolt of electricity. Finally I reached the end of the questions, but MASTER JOHN insisted that we run through them again to make sure I hadn't lied. We repeated the test five times and on the sixth try I passed without one small zap of juice. Here are my answers, for I know them still;

"MASTER it is called piggy MASTER.

"MASTER piggy is a slave MASTER.

"MASTER piggy's duties are to serve its MASTERS at all times MASTER.

"MASTER piggy is the lowest form of life on earth MASTER

"MASTER, piggy has no rights or privileges other than those given to it by its MASTERS.

"MASTER piggy has no choice in what it does. It will obey any and all commands of its MASTERS.

"MASTER piggy will worship its MASTERS at all times MASTER.

"MASTER, piggy loves and worships only its MASTERS.

"MASTER, piggy owns nothing, everything it has is the property of its MASTERS.

"MASTER, piggy is the property of its MASTERS to do with as they please.

"MASTER piggy will devote the rest of its life to pleasing its MASTERS.

By the final run through this shit head slave (for that is how I thought of myself from then on) could repeat these statements clearly, distinctly and with total honesty of belief.   Piggy was indeed a slave.

Chapter 13. The Club

This dumb fuck cop slave was released from the lie detector chair and it immediately fell to its hands and knees in front of its MASTERS.

MASTER JOHN spoke again. "There are many rules and regulations which slaves must follow piggy and to break any of these rules means severe punishment. We will teach you most of them as we go along but tell us now those rules that you have been taught."

"MASTER piggy is not to speak unless spoken to SIR. MASTER piggy will always treat its MASTERS with the respect and reverence due to their position SIR. MASTER piggy will obey every order given to it SIR. MASTER............" but try as it may this dumb ass slave couldn't think of any other orders that had been given it.

MASTER JOHN said, "Good for a beginning piggy. You will be receiving other orders with time. Now Denny I believe you had something you wanted to give to piggy."

MASTER DENNY was in front of this shit slave, his hands on his hips, his tight latex pants rolled down so that his massive black cock hung out. "Hey shit head, look at me and open your mouth." This asshole slave did as ordered, looking up at the black MASTER and opening its mouth wondering what was to happen. MASTER DENNY took his huge dick in his hand, aimed it at this stupid fuck's face and let go with a heavy, steady stream of hot steamy piss. Most of it went into this piss drinking slave's mouth but some splashed in its face and dripped to the floor. This fucked up slave couldn't believe that one man could have so much piss in him and had to struggle to keep its mouth open for the length of time it took MASTER DENNY to empty his bladder. But eventually the stream dried up into a few drops and MASTER DENNY shook his cock and put it back into his pants.

MASTER JOHN said, "Piggy another rule is that whenever anyone is kind enough to give you something, you must always thank them for it. Now thank Denny for the gift and then lick up the piss on the floor that you missed."

"MASTER DENNY thank you SIR for letting this dumb fuck slave drink your piss SIR." MASTER DENNY grunted something while this slave lowered its face to floor and began licking up the small pools of piss that had missed its mouth.

"Well piggy I think it is time that we brought you out to the club and let our customers see you," Master John said. "Of course the problem is that there just might be some undercover cops out there looking for reasons to close us down. So we have to obey all the laws. One of which is that no one can show his private parts in public. In other words piggy, we can't let you out there as you now are and as you will be most of the time you are with us. So we have this pair of latex briefs for you to wear."

With that MASTER JOHN handed this slave a pair of black latex briefs and ordered it to put them on. This was an even harder job than removing the slave's boots had been hours ago. This slave's body was wet from sweat and piss and pulling the tight rubber up this slave's legs and around its crotch and ass was difficult But finally this slave succeeded and its private parts were covered, barely, by rubber. The rear of the briefs, the part covering this slave's ass, had a small curly tail attached – a tail very similar to what a pig has.

Next this slave was given a rubber hood to wear because, as MASTER JOHN said, "we don't want piggy immediately identified by anyone out there even if it does look a bit different from when it first arrived here. You never know who might spot him for the stupid, fuck cop who used to harass us. Also piggy you just might see some of your fellow cops out there enjoying themselves." The hood was in the shape of a pig, with a round flat nose and small pointed ears. It fit tightly over this slave's shaved head and down its neck. A thick rubber collar was then locked on this slave's neck which effectively kept the hood in place. This shit head slave began almost immediately sweating in the rubber. A leash was attached to the collar and with MASTER JOHN holding one end this fucked up pig slave was led on its hands and knees out the door and into the club itself.

Chapter 14. **The Tub**

There was a lot of talking and noise in the club when we first entered, this pig slave on its hands and knees being led by a leash, but it stopped and total silence ensued as we walked through. This slave knew that everyone there was looking at it as it crawled past them so it hung its head in shame and humiliation. MASTER JOHN was greeting various men and stopped periodically to talk with friends. When this happened pig slave just kept its eyes to the floor, generally looking at a variety of leather boots being worn by the customers. The noise level slowly picked up again with some whistling at piggy and a couple even venturing to touch the new slave. MASTER JOHN tugged at piggy's leash and led it into what piggy was able to recognize from the smell and tile floor, as the club's toilet area. This slave was led to one corner of the room where a large metal tub- like vat was located.

MASTER JOHN said, "Get in the tub piggy" and this slave climbed over the edge of the tub and sat down in the metal tub. "Lie on your back piggy and put your hands up over your pig head." This pig slave did as it was ordered and felt MASTER JOHN attach metal cuffs to piggy's wrists, fastening them to the wall above. "Stretch down completely piggy and spread your legs. Good pig. Now piggy this is our piss tub, a place for our customers to get rid of all the beer they've been drinking all night. You are very lucky because you are going to be able to give our customers the pleasure of pissing on you while you are here. You'll like that won't you piggy?"

"MASTER, yes MASTER piggy will like that MASTER."

"Good pig," Master John stated, sounding proud. "And remember piggy whenever anyone gives you anything you must thank them for it. Do you understand?"

'MASTER yes MASTER."

"Clever little pig," Master John laughed. "Ok, I'll be the first since I need to relieve myself." And with that MASTER JOHN pulled out his cock and let a stream of hot piss pour out on to this slave's stomach and chest. This pig slave just lay there staring at its MASTER and when MASTER JOHN was finished, piggy said, "Thank you MASTER JOHN for sharing your piss with slave piggy."

"Well, piggy MASTER has work to do and things to take care of, but I think you'll be comfortable enough here. Enjoy yourself and remember to thank people."

He left but was soon followed by a long line of men in various degrees of leather, rubber, uniforms and boots. Each in turn pissed on the stretched out body of this former haughty cop. And after each man had finished this asshole slave thanked him loudly, causing a number of them to laugh and a few to even say "you're welcome pig". This pig slave studied the men pissing on it and did indeed recognize a couple of fellow officers from the department. One, a well built Italian man had been in the police academy with piggy and this slave was surprised to see him in head to toe leather, a black cigar in his mouth and a huge cock that he took pride in aiming directly at piggy's face. This fucked up slave realized that he would never be able to look this man in the eyes again; even though the other cop had no idea who it was he was pissing on.

The line of men pissing on the slave seemed endless and this dumb fucker soon realized that the tub had no drainage to it and that it was slowly filling up with piss. Piggy heard a couple of the men in line talking, saying that there was a contest on to see if they could fill the tub completely so that only the slave's head was above the piss line. Piggy believed this was happening when it began to recognize faces of men who had pissed on it earlier. They were drinking, pissing on the slave, returning to the bar and drinking even more beer, then pissing again.

Chapter 15. *Cleanup*

This shit for brains slave had no conception of time and didn't know how long it was actually in the piss tub, but it heard the last call gong go off when the piss level was splashing over its legs and stomach. With the sound of that last call and for the next half hour or so the line seemed to get longer and the intensity of the piss pouring on piggy's body was stronger. Although piggy was not totally covered with piss when the last customer shook the final drops from his cock, much of it was submerged in the warm liquid.

This pig slave could hear the sound of the men in the other room slowly subside and then MASTER MIKE came into the toilet. "Ah piggy shit, I haven't had the opportunity to add my donation to your cause, but I'll do that now." And with that MASTER MIKE pulled out his cock and let go a hard stream of steamy piss directly into piggy's face. When he finished, this slave said, "Thank you MASTER MIKE for sharing your piss with piggy SIR."

MASTER MIKE laughed and then undid the cuffs which were attached to the slave's wrists. "OK, shit head, get out of the tub and step over here to the showers. Damn but you stink boy, gotta clean you off."

Before it could shower MASTER MIKE showed piggy where the plug for the piss tub was located and this slave had to reach in, pull the plug and watch the liquid swirl down a drain. This pig slave was then handed a pail, told to fill it with water and wash down the inside of the tub so that it was thoroughly clean. It took slave piggy 20 minutes to get the tub clean enough for MASTER MIKE'S approval. Then this pig slave was led to what turned out to be a shower stall and told to stand under it. MASTER MIKE turned on the faucets and a forceful stream of ice cold water poured down on this miserable piss covered pig slave who had all it could do to tolerate what felt like thousands of sharp needles puncturing its skin. Piggy had to stand under the water for an incredibly long period protected from the ice cold spray only by the latex hood and briefs. At times the cold water stung almost as badly as the electricity had earlier. When MASTER MIKE finally turned off the water, slave piggy was shivering and numb from the cold. MASTER MIKE tossed the slave a rough towel and ordered it to dry itself off. The towel was the most coarse material this slave has ever felt and rubbing it over its tender skin felt more like using sand paper and caused even more pain.

Finally MASTER MIKE said it was enough and led the slave into the main room of the club where this slave was ordered to go around the room, picking up glasses and beer bottles. This slave then had to put all the chairs on to the tables and sweep the floor. The twins were still behind the bar and one of the said to this slave, "Hey shit head, get used to this because one of your jobs will be to keep this place clean."

"Yes SIR, thank you SIR" was an automatic answer from this slave and the twins just laughed.

Chapter 16. *Master John*

Finally after the club room and bar had been swept and cleaned, this slave was let into the back room which piggy slave realized was set up like a dungeon with iron cages on the floor, crosses, a rack there too. On the wall hung a variety of whips, shackles, cuffs, leather, rubber, and iron hoods, and other torture devices which slave piggy didn't immediately recognize. Slave piggy was ordered to remove its briefs and then kneel beside a thick padded mat on the floor and to stay there until it received other orders.

This slave did as ordered, but as it knelt there it realized that it was exhausted and that it could easily lay on the mat and fall asleep, but it knew that if it did the punishment would be severe. So piggy the cop slave just knelt there, its head in the rubber pig hood that seemed now to be a part of it and waited.

After a few minutes MASTER JOHN came in and stood before this slave. Piggy's first reaction was to begin licking MASTER JOHN'S leather boots but MASTER pulled them away. "No need for that now Piggy. You'll have plenty of time in the future to spit shine all our boots and show them the respect they deserve. But now I think it is my turn to explore that body of yours, especially that ass. My cock is anxious to probe your cunt. Would you like that piggy?"

"Yes MASTER JOHN, piggy would be very pleased to have you fuck this ass MASTER."

MASTER JOHN chuckled and then began removing his shirt exposing a well developed, hairy chest. "Up on the mat slave," Master John ordered. Piggy did as ordered and soon the bare chested MASTER was lying beside it. The MASTERS hands began exploring this pig's body, fingering and gently caressing every inch of it from the slave's neck, to its armpits to its chest, its stomach and hips. When MASTER reached slave's crotch he laughed and said, "Ah piggy I see this turns you on." And he was right because this pig slave was as hard as it had ever been. "Well, pig, slaves aren't allowed to cum without their MASTERS permission and you don't have that permission so I better not even see the smallest drop of pre cum or you're in trouble boy."

MASTER JOHN lay on top of this slave and without even thinking this slave began licking its MASTERS chest and sucking on his nips. This slave heard its MASTER moan and knew it was a moan of contentment and that the slave was doing the right thing. MASTER JOHN then lay on his back and ordered piggy to make oral love to the bulge in the leather pants of his crotch. This slave had no trouble kissing the heavy leather and sucking on the hard shape of the cock that lurked behind it. Before it realized just what it was doing, this slave began using its teeth to undo MASTERS belt and the top button of his pants. This slave heard MASTER whisper, "Yes pig, get my cock free." Piggy used its teeth to pull down MASTERS zipper and separate the pants so that the beautiful cock sprung out. And piggy immediately began licking the cock head and then the shaft just as it had been taught many hours before. Piggy was lost in its desire to suck on that cock and was shocked when MASTER JOHN suddenly pulled it from his throat.

"On your back pig," he said. This slave did as ordered and soon felt that shaft gently sliding into its ass. It was an easy, gentle penetration but soon this slave felt the shaft filling more and more of him as MASTER JOHN worked it in and out of slave's body. A fleeting thought went through this slave's brain that there was no pain in this, only a warm fulfilling pleasure. But the thought passed as this slave worked its body in rhythm with its MASTER. The eruption inside its ass was explosive and highly satisfying. This slave heard itself cry out in pleasure as its MASTER emptied his jizz into its ass.

MASTER JOHN lay on top of this slave for a time even though he no longer was inside the slave's body. Whispering in the slave's ear, MASTER told it how happy he was that this pig had chosen to be their slave and that he knew Piggy would work hard to always please its MASTERS. Piggy was confused at first but the more MASTER JOHN played with its body and whispered in its ear, piggy knew that yes it did indeed want to be this man's slave and bring him pleasure.

Chapter 17. *To Bed*

MASTER JOHN stood up, pulled up his pants and ordered the slave to remain there until MASTER DENNY came back. This slave thought then that each of its MASTERS would want to have sex with it but somehow this didn't upset it. However this was not to be because when MASTER DENNY arrived he led piggy to one of the cages and ordered the slave to lie in it on its stomach with its arms and legs stretched out to the side where they were locked in place with leather restraints. When the door to the cage was closed and locked, this slave's head was placed through an opening in it... A shelf with rubber padding was there for piggy to rest its head. Piggy thanked MASTER DENNY for this privilege. MASTER DENNY just laughed and said, "Shit you fuck ass. That isn't there for your convenience, its there for us. We want your mouth available in case we have to take a piss during the night and we don't want to bother unlocking your cage. In fact I have to get rid of some beer right now, so let me raise you up to a more reachable level and let you have it."

With that MASTER DENNY began pulling on some chains which this pig slave soon realized were attached to the cage and soon it was hanging about 3 feet off the ground. "Perfect," MASTER DENNY said, "now open that toilet mouth of yours asshole."

Piggy slave did as ordered and soon was drinking more hot, steamy piss directly out of MASTER DENNYS cock. When he finished and after this slave had thanked him he said, "Ok shit head, one more present for you and then I'm off till tomorrow afternoon. Mike has the duty tonight so you won't be totally alone your first night here."

This slave's body lay flat against the bottom bars of the hanging cage with its wrists and ankles tightly fastened to the sides and its cock and balls hanging down through the bars. MASTER DENNY reached under the cage and this slave soon realized that the MASTER had tied its balls and attached a weight to it.

"Hey shit head," he said, "that's not your boot tied to your balls, just an old sneaker someone left here once. But it will do. I just don't recommend that you swing this cage too much tonight 'cause when you do the sneak is gonna swing too and that could become a problem for you. Good night fucker, see you tomorrow."

This slave just lay there in the cage, uncomfortable and hurting but exhausted and soon found itself dozing off. Then MASTER MIKE came in.

"Ah piggy, you're looking good, for a pig that is. I'll be sleeping in the next room and will be able to see and hear you so I wouldn't try to leave if I were you. Not that I think you could. Now open your mouth pig and let me piss before I hit the sack. Then I have another gift for you."

As with MASTER DENNY this slave thanked MASTER MIKE for the gift of his piss and wondered what the other gift would be. MASTER MIKE wheeled in a table with a TV and a VCR on it and plugged it in. "I thought you might enjoy seeing this movie I made pig. The acting isn't very good and some of the dialogue is a little stilted, but I think you should enjoy it." He turned on the set and soon the images appeared. It showed a big, tough motorcycle cop coming into a room. This slave watched fascinated at the highly edited film which showed the downfall of this former cop. It was edited in such a way as to lead the viewer into believing that this slave had willingly gone through the ordeals of the night.

Piggy dozed off and on throughout the night listening to itself tell its MASTERS how much it wanted to suck their cocks and be their slave and watching itself gladly have and seemingly enjoy sex with other men. Piggy knew then for certain that there was no backing out and that it could never be anything but a slave to these MASTERS.

Will piggy have further adventures?

THE PRICE

Written by: Dutch Roberts

Jason knew he shouldn't have had those last two celebratory glasses of champagne before he got into his car to head home, but, he was in such a good mood and it just seemed so right at the time, that he went for it. Contracts, such as the one he just signed, didn't happen everyday.

However, now, behind the wheel of his car, he realized that it wasn't such a great idea after all. Thankfully, it was late at night, so the streets of London and, in particular, Soho were rather devoid of traffic. Although, it still wasn't safe to be driving around slightly intoxicated, so as soon as he saw a side street to pull off into he took it.

Sliding into a parking space on the quiet street Jason put his sporty, compact, silver car into park and quickly killed the engine. Withdrawing the keys he twirled them on his index finger for a few seconds before dropping them into one of the deep pockets of his heavy cashmere overcoat.

"Well, where am I?" he found himself asking the cold, quiet winter evening around him as he glanced out the side window of his quickly cooling car, eyeing the street up and down.

I guess I should figure this out and walk my ass home, he thought to himself as he prepared for his departure from the car.

Taking his leather gloves and cashmere scarf from the seat next to him he slid both on and proceeded to step out into the chilled night. Standing next to his car he looked around, deciding the best way to proceed from his current position. It appeared that he was on Brewer Street, which meant he wasn't all that far from his flat. He would probably be home and in bed in less than 20 minutes.

Focusing on the sidewalk ahead he began to walk. After a few steps, he casually glanced at the thick, silver watch that hung heavily on his wrist, slowly deciphering the slightly blurred numbers on the face.

"After midnight," Jason muttered, turning up the collar on his coat and adjusting the scarf around his neck.

With only the sound of his expensive dress shoes clicking on the sidewalk, he suddenly became alarmed when he heard a second set mirroring his own, stepping in time – stopping as he stopped – obviously following him! Glancing over his shoulder, he became even more paranoid as he was unable to see anyone on his tail.

Calm down Jay, he told himself, *it's nothing. You had a little too much to drink and your mind is…*

Returning his gaze before him, he stopped dead in his tracks, as his thoughts were abruptly interrupted, along with his progression down the street.

"Well, if it isn't Mr. Blond, Blue, and Beautiful," the leather-clad man before him snarled, his unshaven, dirty face mere inches from Jason's own.

Startled, Jason thought of pulling back, but instead he only drunkenly staggered to the side a bit, caught off guard by this sudden confrontation.

"Going somewhere?" the filthy man questioned, as he advanced forward, brandishing a metal baseball bat.

"Uh, listen, I don't want any trouble...," Jason sputtered, placing all of his attention on the bat, unaware that the guy was swiftly backing him into a dark corner as he advanced.

"Oh, is that so? Well, then, you shouldn't be out and about on a cold night like this, wandering the streets alone," the man spat in return. "And, after all, Jason, I'm not gonna hurt ya. I'm gonna help ya."

"Oh?" Jason replied, unable to imagine how this disgusting man knew his name, unless he was a member of...

"Yes, because you see, Jason, I'm one of your biggest fans!"

With that, the bat came swiftly into view and, sadly enough, it was the last thing Jason remembered seeing before he blacked out.

Awaking with a start Jason was relieved to find himself still clothed and unbound. He was somewhere inside and still had on his smartly tailored, three-piece, navy-colored suit, with matching tie and pocket square. His leather dress shoes and silk socks were still in place, as was, obviously, his crisp, white dress shirt with its French cuffs and wide spread collar. He actually didn't look all that bad, all things considered.

"Ok, get up," a voice directed from behind where Jason lay, which he quickly realized was a somewhat unkempt, single bed rammed into the corner of a very dilapidated room.

Looking to see his assailant, Jason turned to make eye contact.

"I said...get up!" the man barked, kicking the side of the bed.

Slowly, Jason did just that and was thankful, even just a little, that his head didn't spin out of control as he stood.

"Now, I want you to come over here and pay attention because I'm only going to say this once...blow me!"

Jason, swiftly taking in his surroundings, caught sight of his top coat that was draped over a simple wooden chair, located in an adjoining alcove of the one room flat he now stood in. A dimly lit, harsh smelling flat that reeked of cheap alcohol, rotting food, and raw body fluids.

"Now, I know you're smarter than this," the man commented, as he stood and lunged at Jason, grabbing him by his arm, forcing him to his knees with great ease.

Jason, looking up from his feeble position, took in the sight of the man before him.

He was massive, but not in the muscular, well-built sense, more in the grotesque, overweight sort of way. His greasy, limp hair framed his unattractive, unwashed face in all the wrong ways, jutting up at odd angles in some places, while sticking to his face in others. The man's unhealthy body was crammed into a pair of ill-fitting leather pants, with matching boots and vest. The leather trench coat that he wore earlier was gone. His scent matched the rooms – foul and nauseating.

"Jason, it would be a shame if I had to beat you several more times with my bat to get you to do what I want," he snarled. "I'm not a violent man. Really, I'm not. But if you push me, I will do what I have to do. It would be a shame to mess up your pretty face and perfect body. I'd like to continue to watch you online after we are finished here, as I'm sure your other fans would like to do as well."

Still in his kneeling position, Jason noticed that the bat wasn't too far out of reach, leaning against the wall, just to their right.

"Now, I'm not going to repeat myself. I refuse!"

Jason, unable to think quickly enough of a way out of the alarming situation – without it turning ugly or brutal – decided to reason with the man, but the moment he opened his mouth, his assailant was barking right over him.

"Please, Jason, let's forgo the bullshit and the flashy smile…and get to work on my cock! I've seen what those luscious lips and that talented mouth can do. Now, get to it."

Jason, growing distraught over the situation, wondered if he could just do as the man asked, finish up quickly, and be on his way. Would this psycho even let him go if he fully cooperated? Did he have a choice? Couldn't he overpower the man and make a break for it? Wasn't that an option? Surely he was stronger than him.

"FUCK!" the man suddenly cursed, as he lunged at Jason again, grabbing him by the deep-blue, silk tie that circled his neck. "I've had it with you!"

With Jason firmly held in place the guy fumbled with his free hand, undoing the snaps on his pants, freeing his fat, slightly soft, raw, uncut cock.

Jason attempted to turn away from the dirty, dripping member, but the guy had him positioned in a way that that was not an option. Here he was, still suited from his photo session, on his knees, about to service the most disgusting man he had ever interacted with in his entire life! It repulsed him to his core.

How is this possible?, his mind screamed, as the man's prick slapped the smooth skin of his cheek.

"Take it bitch! Just like you do in those movies you make!" the man moaned, as he pushed and shoved his growing member against Jason's face. "I know you enjoy sucking cock! I saw you take Fred's like an absolute pro!"

Jason's mind whirled, as the man pushed and shoved and forced himself onto him.

"Listen, Jay, I didn't want to have to use this as a bargaining chip, but…," he paused now, making sure he had Jason's full attention. When it was clear he did, he continued, "I saw how you ran that kid over in your car. That is why you pulled over, several blocks away from the accident, right? You were going to head back to make sure he was ok, right? That would have been the right thing to do. No?"

Jason looked up with an expression of pure horror on his usually serene face. What this guy was saying was impossible! He hadn't hit anyone! He was lying! He had to be!

"Oh, I know what you're thinking, so let me show you these," the man calmly noted, as he held his grip on Jason's tie, twisting and directing him toward a computer screen on a desk to their left.

With an abrupt click of the mouse, a slide show of photos snapped into view. The slideshow contained images of Jason leaving the offices where he worked. There, before his eyes, were pictures of him, behind the wheel of his car, driving recklessly. To his surprise, there were shots of him blasting through red lights and cutting corners. To his horror, there were images of…

Oh God, no! his mind cried out, as he looked upon the twisted, seemingly lifeless body of a young boy, lying in the street.

"See, now, I wouldn't attempt to do anything stupid or not do everything I ask of you, because, ya see, Jay, I have proof that you did a runner," the man's lips curled into a wicked smile as he calmly noted this to Jason. "It seems my time has finally come. After months of waiting and watching you handed me the perfect scenario, one I've been dreaming of ever since I saw your first spread back in 2005."

Jason suddenly felt sick to his stomach, as if he were going to vomit. So much so, that he could feel the hot bile building in his throat.

"Aw, you don't look too good, Jay. Perhaps some cock will brighten your disposition."

With that, the guy shoved his raw, dirty cock deep into Jason's slightly gaping mouth. The taste and smell of it made Jason gag. It made the juices in his stomach churn. It caused him to choke and groan, suddenly feeling lightheaded, as if he could pass out any second.

Thrusting in and out, the guy was relentless, moaning and grunting wildly with each power thrust. "Yeah! That's right boy! Suck it!" he bellowed, holding Jason's head with one hand and his tie with the other, as he drilled his throat. "My pretty little suited slut! You fuckin' cock whore! Look at you go!"

The seconds turned into minutes, which turned into what felt like an eternity to Jason as his face was brutally fucked.

"Hey, let me ask ya, did your boss pick out your handsome outfit? Huh? You can tell me," the guy casually questioned, as he continued to thrust his throbbing rod deeper into Jason's throat. "It's a real pretty suit. Do you get to keep it? It would be a damn shame to fuck it up, if ya did get to take this home with ya, but, oh well, what the hell do I care!?"

With that, he reached down and yanked on the perfectly tailored breast pocket that still sported an artistically folded, silk pocket square.

RIP!

"Aw, look what happened, Jay! I guess you won't be returning this particular suit to the office," the guy smirked as he continued to firmly hold Jason's face in place, thrusting in and out.

"Damn, you know what…I had a few too many beers myself this evening. Right before we magically crossed paths as a matter of fact. So, you know what that means, right?"

Jason's eyes widened, as it was all too clear what this pig planned to do to him. Struggling, he made every attempt to break free of the man's hold, but, somehow, the guy had a rock solid, unforgiving grip on his head.

Within seconds, the scorching hot, golden-yellow liquid was filling Jason's throat and stomach. Again, he felt on the verge of vomiting, as the hot juice saturated his insides. Struggling, he continued to make every effort to break free, until, the guy suddenly released him!

Falling back on his haunches, gasping for air – tasting nothing but the hot urine on his lips and tongue – Jason could do nothing but cry out and moan, as the foul flow continued to shoot from the man's erect cock.

Striking him dead in the face, the neck, across his silk tie, onto his waistcoat, all over his bright shirt, and down into the crotch of his navy dress pants, he was soon slick, from head to toe in the hot fluid.

"Aw, now look what you made me do. I was just going to let you drain me, but you had to go and pull away," the guy lamented, as if he truly meant it. "Your a mess!"

Jason, stunned into silence, sat for several minutes, letting the piss soak in, as well as drip from his face. His body shuddered at the sensation and scent.

"Ok, get up," the guy directed, motioning with his strong hands.

Jason, unable to move, remained in his place, on the floor, only glaring up at his assailant with his blue eyes.

"Come on. Don't look at me like that. You know what you are. You're a cock whore and we both know that. So do all the men who have seen you on the net. Well, all of them who are still alive, that is, unlike the young bloke you killed tonight," the man droned on now, as he subconsciously stroked his still exposed, dripping cock. "Now, get up!"

Jason, realizing that he was in a situation that was far beyond his control, stood before the man in his piss slick suit.

Approaching Jason, the man reached forward and took a hold of his damp, silk tie, yanking on it until their faces were mere inches apart.

"You realize you're ass is mine," the guy whispered, as his hot, rancid breath washed over Jason's face.

Remaining silent Jason only scowled at the filthy beast before him.

"Ok, let's get this little party really going," the man noted now, as he let go of the tie. "Turn around."

Jason slowly did as he was told, wondering what would be done to him next. There were so many possibilities and every single one of them caused his body to go sour with dread.

Soon, he felt the guy's hands all over his body, focusing mostly on his backside and in particular, his ass. Groping and caressing, the guy remained focused on this act for several minutes, until finally, Jason heard and felt…

RIP!

Suddenly, and rather violently, the seat of his pants was torn open, exposing the pale blue, cotton briefs within.

"Very nice. Did the guys select your undergarments as well?"

The massaging and manhandling continued; as the guy ran his grubby hands over the exposed area, until…

RIP!

Jason, unable to take the abuse any longer bolted for the door before him. He couldn't take it anymore, but little did he realize the man must have sensed his overwhelming desire to abandon the flat. As Jason lunged for the door the guy managed to get a firm grip on his suit jacket, so that as he attempted to propel himself forward, he was, instead, suddenly flying through the air backward with several stitches of his jacket splitting along the way.

Stumbling, and falling to the hardwood floor below, Jason hit the ground hard, feeling the wind knocked from his lungs, but, something in him snapped and he decided that if he had to claw his way to the door and out of this hellhole, he would, regardless of what the man had captured on film.

Struggling the entire way, Jason attempted a brave fight across the floor, as he groped his way toward the door, but he quickly realized his efforts were futile, as the heavyset man lunged at him and landed on top of him, pinning him to the floor.

Their bodies clashed and entwined, rolling across the floor, as the attacker continued to gain the upper hand, pinning Jason repeatedly.

"Give up!" he cried, as he held Jason in place with his exposed cock mere inches from its desired resting place, which was perfectly exposed through the torn fabric of Jason's suit pants.

Bucking wildly under the guy's hold Jason grunted and moaned, attempting to give his best fight, until, finally, he gave in. He fell silent and still, allowing himself to be defeated and overpowered. The fight was out of him.

"There, now, isn't that better?"

Slowly, the guy stood, but not before he reached down and worked Jason's silk tie off from around his neck, leaving it tied in its Windsor knot. Pulling his wrists behind his back, the guy utilized the silk accessory to bind Jason. Satisfied with his work, he stood back now and eyed up his prize.

"You truly are one beautiful man and I'm sorry that we couldn't have met under better circumstances, but, such is life," the man muttered, continuing to stroke his cock. "Now, you may think I'm an animal and, well, at times I can be, but, listen up Jay, because I'm going to tell you something that will make you very happy."

Jason, in his prone position, in the middle of the floor, wasn't sure anything would make him 'happy' at this point, but he was willing to listen.

"I'm going to fuck your ass, Jay. Got that? There is no way around it. I need to be inside of you and feel my load explode in your ass, but – and this is the 'happy' part – I will indeed use a rubber as I do this. Ok?"

Jason, not sure what the man was expecting his reaction to be, remained silent in his bound position.

"Ok, here goes," the man calmly noted as he removed a condom from his pants pocket and worked it onto his throbbing prick.

Slowly, with measured steps the man moved into position, working his cock toward Jason's prone hole.

"Please, no, don't…," Jason cried out, but it was too late, the man was intent on claiming his long awaited prize.

Inch by inch the man's tool slid into Jason's smooth, muscular hole. Inch by inch, it invaded his anus, filling him up.

"Dear, God!" Jason moaned, as he felt it penetrate his body.

"Oh, like you've never done this before!" the man grunted, as he slid his entire member into Jason. This was quickly followed by powerful thrusts, in and out, in and out.

"NO!"

"Yes, my dear boy, fuckin' yes!" the man replied in return, drilling deeper and deeper.

Soon, within the piss soaked suit, Jason's body began to overheat and soak the material with his manly sweat. His once crisp dress shirt became mostly transparent, clinging to his torso like a second skin. His briefs became moist and clingy as well, plastered to his cock and balls.

Repeatedly, the man fucked him. Wildly, he used the suited form below him as a toy, until finally, with a seemingly unending moan and a thrashing of his body he exploded inside the condom, inside Jason's ass.

"FUCK!"

Jason remained in place as the man withdrew his still throbbing, latex coated cock.

"There, see, every drop contained in one place," the man calmly stated as he motioned to the seed filled rubber dangling off the end of his meat, but then, with one grand gesture he ripped it from his body and tossed it at Jason's coat that was sitting nearby.

"Aw, I'm sorry, I guess I got some on your pretty cashmere coat," the man chuckled. "What a shame."

Jason, stricken and disgusted continued to lie upon the hardwood floor. As he remained in his place volatile anger began to develop deep within his body. He wanted to lash out and destroy this man, as well as the evidence that he was holding against him.

"Now, don't get any smart ideas," the man noted as he walked to the bed in the corner and lit a fag, taking a good, long hit on it before expelling the smoke through his nose.

Slowly, Jason regained the ability to move and even managed to free his tie-bound hands. Standing, he scowled at the man, a powerful rage playing across his normally angelic face.

"Again, don't think for one minute you can report me, or take revenge, or whatever it is that your pretty little mind is formulating as a plan right now. I have the upper hand and you know it," the man stated before taking another long drag.

Jason, feeling filthy and used stood silently.

Standing, the man walked toward Jason and with a flick of his fag shot ashes at him. Then, as if that wasn't enough he took the lit end and rubbed it into the lapel of Jason's suit jacket.

"Aw, you sure make one sad looking ashtray," the man noted as he flicked the butt at Jason's cum soaked coat.

Jason, still stunned, remained in his place, his mind slowly going numb. The anger, once growing inside of him, subsided and turned into a cold, quiet loathing.

Deciding that he wasn't finished with Jason the leather pig reached out and began to pluck the polished buttons from not only his suit jacket, but the vestment within.

PLINK.

PLINK.

PLINK.

PLINK.

PLINK.

The buttons tinkered across the floor, rolling into corners, and under the slim furnishings of the flat.

"You look like you've really given in," the man commented now, taking in the deadened look upon Jason's face. "That's a shame. Perhaps this will help."

Reaching for the front of Jason's dress shirt the man tore it open, sending more buttons to the four corners of the room. Soon, he had him exposed to his waist, his well-defined, slightly hairy pecs and abs revealed.

"Damn, even better in person," the man exclaimed, tugging on a nip, "but I'm going to save the rest for next time. I wouldn't want to use you all up in one fling, because, you see Jay, you will be coming back. Very soon, I would think."

"No," Jason whispered.

"Yes, indeed you will, because I'm not finished with you. We still have a lot to explore. For example, I really didn't get to enjoy this suit of yours as I should have. I guess I got lost in the moment and the desire to fuck your hot ass. You would think I would have planned this much better."

"Please...," Jason muttered.

"Oh, please nothing," the man replied, "and perhaps I'll invite a few friends over too, when you return, suited to the nines."

"What?"

"Oh, didn't I tell you. I want you to come back, but next time I want you in that tux that you wore for that shoot that you did a few weeks ago. You remember the one. No?"

"But...I can't," Jason begged now.

"Why not? I'm sure that set of formal wear is sitting around those offices somewhere, very much unworn. The men won't notice if you borrow it. Their focus is on the suits, one missing tux won't matter to them. Besides, they'll just buy a new one when they need it."

Confused, angered, and distraught, Jason felt overwhelmed now, unable to fathom how long this torture would continue. How could he get out of this? How could he escape this nightmare? Would begging and bribing this slob work?

"Oh, and, all the pleading and money in the world won't save you from this predicament," the man coolly noted, as if reading Jason's mind. Then, he quickly added, "I want you to put on your coat and get out now. I'm finished with you."

"But…," Jason stammered, motioning to his soiled and torn garments.

"What? I think you look perfect! I want you to remember this evening, just the way you are, because, after all Jay, you need to understand, there certainly is a price to the fame you have acquired."

Disgusted, Jason swiftly slid into his coat – with its obvious stains – and raced for the door, only pausing on the threshold when he heard the man calling to him.

"Oh, Jay, don't worry, you can hardly see the rip in your pants. The coat covers it up nicely. And, by the way, it will be crystal clear when I want you to return. Trust me."

Departing, Jason didn't look back. He didn't look back at all, not even when he was once again safe in his car, racing off to his home – far more sober than earlier in the evening.

The man, sitting for a while, thinking over the events of the evening, soon considered lighting up another fag, but decided against it and, turning to his computer clicked the slideshow off.

"Damn, that was almost too easy," he muttered, as he clicked on folders and files found on his desktop.

Quickly finding the batch of photos he was casually looking for he sat back in his chair and smiled.

"Poor bloke," the man lamented, "Doesn't he know the first thing about the power of computers and digital manipulation?"

Looking at the archive of pictures he rolled the mouse over several. There, before him, were the unaltered pictures of Jason *not* running anyone down with his car. He wasn't even close, but, in his intoxicated state, he himself couldn't remember the truth. He couldn't remember and wouldn't remember, not doing what the altered pictures showed him doing.

"Damn, I'm good," he barked aloud to himself as he clicked the computer off. "Too damn good."

With that, he got up from his desk and sauntered into the tiny bathroom, located just off the single – recently rented – room.

Standing before the sink, he began to remove the rather expensive and utterly impressive disguise he had utilized to complete his elaborate plot. Layer by layer, piece by piece, he unveiled himself, able to see his true form once again.

"Man, when you take on a new project, you really do go all the way," the man, known to most as Dutch or Mr. Roberts, marveled to his reflection. "All...the...way," he repeated, with a wicked grin.

THE GUY NEXT DOOR

Written by: Ron Bossman

Wayne and I have been living next door to each other for about 10 years. He's a great guy. There isn't a weekend that goes by that doesn't find either me over his house to watch the game or vice versa. Our wives get along great as well. They are always going shopping together. Hell, they even have gone on "girls' weekends" together down to Vegas. It was during one of those weekends that my current situation began.

No actually it really began at the gym about a month ago. You see Wayne and I have always been very competitive. We each have to have the best lawn equipment. The best work tools. It's almost a challenge between us. We try to outdo each other when it comes to everything. We live side by side right on the edge of a Town forest. The yards back up to a wooded area of town. When Wayne put a pool in two summers ago I had to out do him and put an even larger pool in. That's how our relationship has been.

We even work out at the same gym together. We get there every morning at 5 A.M. rain or shine. We are always trying to push each other and reach new limits to what we can do. Wayne's a great buddy. We both flatter ourselves at being over 40 and still being able to wear our college jeans. Wayne's a couple of inches taller than I am. At 6' and 220 you'd think I was good sized. Wayne is 6'2 and at least 240 but still has a 48" chest and a 34" waist. It was right after our morning work out that it happened. The locker room was kind of quiet being a Friday morning and all. We had a good hard workout, chest and abs. We both hit the showers. I had been noticing how ripped Wayne was getting lately. He was more defined now than I had ever seen him. I was taking a good look while he was showering across the shower room. There was no one else there, thank God. My mind sort of got away from me. I was noticing how he had soaped up his entire body. It looked great on him. Wayne was a really furry guy. His legs were like tree trunks. He had this V shape to his back from all the lat work we had been doing. He was looking real good. It was then that I noticed my dick starting to get hard. Once it started I couldn't stop it. It took on a mind of its own. There was this one very uncomfortable moment when Wayne's eyes met mine. He caught me staring at him. He immediately looked down at my erection. It all happened in about 20 seconds. I turned quickly. Switched the water over to ice cold and hoped that would get rid of my erection. I stayed in the shower longer than usual waiting for Wayne to leave first so I could give my dick a chance to get soft again. I was praying that he hadn't really noticed.

Wayne couldn't get his mind off of what happened that morning at the gym. He had been thinking about it all day at work. Steve had been a buddy of his for years. He really enjoyed the time they spent together. Their morning workout routine was the highlight of his day. He enjoyed being with Steve. Steve was a little shorter than Wayne. About 6' but really built. A nice firm body covered in fur just like him. Steve had done a lot of work on his body thanks to their morning routines and it showed. Lately he had been noticing Steve trying to steal glances at him in the shower. This morning he caught Steve almost in a trance with a huge erection just staring at him. The funny thing was Wayne liked it. Good thing Steve turned around as soon as he realized what he was doing. Wayne also started to get a hard on. He shut the water off real quick and went to grab a towel and head back to get dressed.

Friday Night

Friday nights are usually a good night to kick back and watch the game. The girls had just left for their weekend in Vegas. We were watching the game in Wayne's basement. We were about half way into the game. Wayne had been restless all night. I could tell he had something on his mind. "Hey Steve we got the whole weekend ahead of us. How about we make a little wager on the game?" Wayne gave me this look that I had never seen on his face before. He was eager and anxious at the same time. I thought about it a few minutes. My team was losing big time but there was a chance it could turn around. "What do you have in mind? You know times have been tough around the house lately with bills and all. Now with this trip the wife has made to Vegas I can't afford much in the way of a wager." I looked over at Wayne. Again with this really eager anxious look on his face. "Let's make it real interesting, forget money. We got the entire weekend and I don't know about you but my list of chores is a mile long. The loser has to do whatever the winner says all weekend. Anything goes." Wayne sort of smiled. I thought about it for a few minutes. Sure would be good if my team won. I'd get Wayne to do all the chores around my house. He did say "anything". My mind started racing. Imagine having an entire weekend of making Wayne do whatever I wanted. "Ok Wayne. You are on." Now I started getting excited. "Great. And just to make sure we are clear anything goes. Right?" Wayne was very specific about this point. "Yeah Wayne. Anything goes. We have a deal." We sat back to watch the game.

—

Wayne's mind was racing as he sat with Steve and watched the game. He couldn't believe he was actually doing this. It was so easy. Steve had gone for it right away. He was thinking of his next step. He had to lay everything out very carefully if this was going to work. He knew he wasn't mistaken. He saw the way Steve tried to steal glances at him while he was in his pool in the back yard or at the gym. He sat back and watched the game.

—

The next few hours were torture. My team did end up coming back. It was real close to the very end. Wayne had this nervous look on his face. I was thinking of all the chores I was going to make Wayne do around my house. It was the last few minutes of the quarter. The score was tied. I watched as Wayne's team scored the winning touchdown. I couldn't believe it. I had lost. Wayne shut the TV off and stood up. "Looks like you lost buddy. You're mine for the weekend." Wayne was smiling from ear to ear. "Yeah I know. Damn, you are going to hold me to this bet?" I know I was whining but I just had to try getting out of it. I had a ton of shit to do around my own house. "I sure am Steve my buddy. As a matter of fact we start right now. Stand up." Wayne was very forceful. He was standing in front of my chair his hands on his hips. He looked very intimidating. "I said stand up." I wasn't sure what was going on but I knew we had a deal fair and square. I stood in front of him. "Wayne, it's almost midnight, there's no way I can do chores this late." I was still very confused. "Steve my buddy, I didn't say anything about chores. Not tonight anyway. The deal was the loser does anything the winner says all weekend. You agreed didn't you." I thought back on what he had said and he was right. We had a deal. "Fine. Ok. What do you want me to do?" Part of me really wanted to submit to Wayne. My mind kept going back to that time in the shower and how hot Wayne looked all soaped up.

My thoughts were brought back to the present moment by Wayne's next command. "Well you can start by taking your clothes off." I laughed. I thought Wayne was kidding with me. Wayne stood there with a serious look on his face. Arms crossed over his chest now. "My clothes? Are you serious?" I asked. Shocked at what he had said but not surprised. I've noticed Wayne taking looks at me in the locker room over the past few months. "Come on Wayne. My clothes?" I asked again. "Look Steve," Wayne said to me. "We had a deal. I haven't gotten any in about a month and you are going to take care of this for me." Wayne grabbed his crotch through his jeans. "All I'm saying is you're going to get me off. You can give me a hand job. But you are getting me off and you will be naked. Now strip." I knew I had agreed to the bet. The problem was the thought of stripping in front of Wayne under these circumstances had started getting me hard. The thought of jacking Wayne off was too much for my mind to handle. My dick started to immediately get hard. I had no idea what was going on in my head at that point.

I kicked my shoes off, and then I pulled my t shirt off over my head. I was standing there in front of Wayne in my jeans and briefs. I knew I was as ripped as him. I was also as hairy as he was. "Is this good? Come on man I'm just going to be jerking you off." I was trying to do anything I could to not take my jeans off. My dick was rock hard at this point. Plus, the wife hadn't done laundry in a while. I had to dig way back in my drawer for underwear and came out with this skimpy pair of bikini briefs the wife got me one Valentines day. They were bright red. There was no way I could let Wayne see me in them.

"I said strip. Take off all of it." Wayne was being very serious and very forceful. I unbuttoned my jeans, unzipped and pulled them off. I was cursing myself for wearing those damned briefs. "What the hell are they?" Wayne was laughing his ass off. "You like wearing these things buddy? And what is this?" First Wayne grabbed the waist band on the skimpy briefs then he grabbed my rock hard dick. It only made matters worse. I was embarrassed on so many levels at this point. "Come on Wayne. Let's get this over with." I said desperately as he handled me. "You didn't answer my question buddy. Why are you hard? Just as hard as last month in the shower." Wayne teased me. I looked at him in shock. My red face now matched the color of my briefs. "Don't deny it Steve. You were rock hard. Is this why?" Wayne grabbed his own dick through his jeans again. "Now take off your briefs." Wayne stood back and watched as I stripped out of my briefs. As I did my cock reached it maximum length and stuck straight up to the ceiling. I was so embarrassed. I immediately covered both my cock and balls with my hands but I'm a big boy. It didn't do much to cover my erection. Again Wayne was laughing his ass off. "You are enjoying this aren't you buddy? Look at how hard you are. Man oh man. This is going to be fun. You stay right there while I go get us a few more beers." I watched as Wayne went into the next room for the beers. I was so embarrassed at this point but very excited as well. My dick was rock hard at the thought of having to jack Wayne off. If I only knew what he had planned for the rest of the weekend.

⌒

Wayne couldn't believe how easy this was all going. He went into the next room for the beers. Steve had fallen right into his trap. The next room was his home office. He kept a fridge stocked with beers for nights when they watched the game. He made sure to keep the lights off so Steve couldn't see in. His computer was turned on but the monitor was shut off. Steve would have no idea what was going on. The new camera Wayne had just bought was pointing right into the next room. Wayne had tested it over the past few days. The position Steve was standing in could easily be captured by his new camera. Everything was going according to plan. He got the beers.

⌒

"Here you go buddy." Wayne tossed me a beer. I opened it and gulped down half the can. I would definitely need this. "Now Steve ole buddy, I want you to unzip me and take my dick out." I hesitated at first. Not moving from where I stood. Beer can still in my hand. "Come on Steve. Get over here and get my dick out." Wayne was serious. I went over to Wayne and reached down unzipping his jeans. I reached in moved past his briefs and pulled out his dick. I had seen it enough times in the shower to know how big Wayne was. I got the monster sized dick out. It already started to grow due to the attention I was giving it. "Now get on your knees in front of it. NOW." Wayne grabbed me by my shoulders and pushed me down to my knees. "Start jerking me off. Nice and slow." I put my hands around Wayne's dick. I could barely close my fist around the shaft. He was so thick and long. My own dick was still as hard as a rock and I was shaking uncontrollably. His dick head was inches from my face. "Hey Steve ole buddy. You sure are hard there. You sure you don't want to suck on it a bit." The thought of sucking on his dick was very exciting but I had never done anything like that before. "No Wayne. Come on man. You said I would just have to jerk you off." I kept jerking up and down on his dick. "Just a taste? Come on Steve. Give it a try. Just your tongue on my head? Come on. What do you say? Give a buddy a break here.

It's been a long time for me." Wayne said in a cajoling tone of voice.

The thought of actually licking and sucking Wayne's dick was too much for me to resist. I had to try it. All those days at the gym watching him in the shower without being able to touch him. Without even knowing what I was doing my tongue was on his dick head. Wayne started to moan. "Yeah buddy. That's it. Lick it good. You like that don't you? You want more don't you?" As if it was someone else responding I heard myself saying "Yes. Oh yeah." Wayne responded quickly. "What was that buddy? You want more of my dick? Let's hear it!" Wayne demanded. I had lost all my inhibitions at that point. "Yah Wayne. I want that dick." I practically shouted. Wayne grabbed me by the back of my head and forced the entire shaft into my mouth and down my throat. I was choking on it. He fucked my face real good. He was gyrating back and forth on my mouth. Still through this entire ordeal I was rock hard. "Fuck Steve. You give a damn good blow job man. Damn good." Wayne continued his assault on my face. He pulled out suddenly. "Stand up Steve. Turn around." Wayne said. "Come on Wayne. You can't do this." I was practically whispering. Wayne came up from behind me and slipped his dick between my legs. He started dry humping me from behind. He forced me to bend over slightly by pushing on my back and shoulders. "Aw fuck Steve that feels real good. You like that buddy? Feel good?" Wayne asked breathlessly. It did feel really hot. I liked the feel of his body against mine. His fur rubbing up against my back. His dick between my legs. "Fuck Wayne. That feels awesome. I've never felt anything like it." I stated. Wayne reached around and grabbed hold of my dick and started jerking me off. It didn't take long for me to get real close to cumming. "Fuck Wayne. I'm going to shoot." I bantered. Wayne was getting close as well. His body started to shake behind me. He started hollering. We both came at the same time.

"That was awesome buddy. How about another beer?" Wayne went in the other room to get us a few beers. He came back with them in hand. "You enjoy that Steve?" I had never felt anything like that before. The orgasm was explosive. I'd be lying if I said no. "Yeah man. It was intense." I said agreeably. Wayne was quick with the response. "Well. Better hit the sack. We have a long weekend ahead of us." "Long weekend?" I asked. "What do you mean?" Wayne reminded me, "Ah buddy. You lost the bet. You are mine for the weekend. I have a list of things for you to do. But first we hit the gym as usual. Be here at 4:45 A.M.

I went to pick up my clothes and get dressed but Wayne stopped me. "No. you ain't getting dressed. You'll stay naked and carry your clothes back with you. "Wayne was standing there. In total control. I had to do his every whim. Embarrassed I carried my clothes as I left his basement through the side door. Our yards connected, it was late, and the yards faced the woods. I was getting hard again as I made my way back to my house naked. I had no idea what tomorrow would bring.

Saturday

I woke up the next morning as usual at 4:30. I didn't need much time to get ready for the gym. I threw on my gym clothes and headed over to Wayne's. My mind kept going back to the night before. Damn that was hot. I had never had an orgasm like that. Never ever. But that couldn't happen again. I would explain to Wayne that I will do whatever chores he had but we couldn't play like last night again. That was a one time thing. It was exactly 4:45 when I knocked on Wayne's door.

Wayne answered pretty quickly. "Hey Steve, sleep well? Ready for a good work out?" Wayne slapped me on the back as I entered the house. "Yeah I am. We're doing legs today right?" Wayne was smiling as he responded. "That's right buddy." I had to clear the air. "Wayne, about last night. I know it was fun and all but that can't happen again. I know I lost the bet and all but no more sex stuff. OK? I will do whatever chores you have but no sex." "Steve, Steve, Steve. I thought you were going to be more cooperative. The bet was anything goes remember? You trying to back out now?" "Wayne I'm serious. NO SEX. We can't do this." I was hoping Wayne would understand and would agree immediately. It wasn't working out that way though. "Steve good buddy. Come downstairs with me for a minute. I have something on my PC I have to show you. "

I followed Wayne downstairs and into his office. The PC was fired up. "Have a seat Steve. Here sit right in my office chair. Can you see the screen ok buddy?" Wayne asked me. "Wayne, what's this all about?" I asked. "I thought we were working out?" "We will, we will. I need you to see something first." Wayne worked the keyboard over my shoulder. Within minutes a video clip was starting. I was shocked at what I saw next. It was actually footage of last night. The clip started with me grabbing a beer from Wayne. I was totally naked. Wayne had captured everything after that point. EVERYTHING.   Only there were a couple of things different about the scene. It took a few minutes for me to realize that the soundtrack wasn't what I remembered. Sure I remember myself saying; "Yah Wayne. I want that dick."; "Fuck Wayne. That feels awesome. I've never felt anything like it." You could hear my voice loud and clear. What was different was what Wayne was saying. Wayne had obviously dubbed his own voice to cover what was actually said. On the clip you could hear Wayne saying. "Steve. I'm not sure we should be doing this. Steve, I don't think this is a good idea." The clip finally ended. I was in shock. I looked up at Wayne. "What the fuck. What's with the clip?" "Let's just call it an insurance policy. You do whatever I say and the clip gets erased. You don't ......well we don't have to go there now." Wayne started to laugh. Frantically I grabbed the keyboard and tried to open the file in order to delete it. Wayne didn't even try to stop me. He just stood there. I successfully deleted the file on his PC. "There. So much for that fucking clip. Thought you had me didn't you?" Wayne just smiled and looked very calm. "I guess I forgot to mention. I've already emailed that clip to my work account. Plus I put a copy of it on a CD which is hidden safely in the house. So, here's the deal Steve good buddy. You do whatever I say whenever I say it or not only does your wife get a copy of the clip on Monday I will e-mail it anonymously to Charlie at work. And guess how long it would be before he spreads the clip around the office?" I sat back in my chair. I knew when I was defeated. I couldn't have my wife seeing that let alone the entire office. "Fine. You win." Wayne stood there with that smile on his face. "Let's hit the gym buddy."

We headed over to the gym in Wayne's car. I couldn't help think of that clip I had just seen. In spite of being mad at Wayne for what he was doing my dick started to stir in my workout pants. Damn that thing had a mind of its own at times. We pulled up to the gym at about 5:15. A little later than usual but we were still some of the first ones there. The gym was usually quiet that early on a Saturday or Sunday morning. We hit the locker room. Wayne hadn't changed into his gym clothes yet. I was ready to go. "Hey Steve. You'll need to change into your gym clothes buddy." I laughed. "I already have them on Wayne. What's with you today?" I started closing up my locker but Wayne stopped me. "No Steve. This is what you'll put on." He handed me a pile of clothes. I looked them over. It was a pair of shorts and a tank top. I practically whispered to him, "Come on Wayne. Don't do this to me. Not in here. Please." My eyes were begging. Wayne just looked directly at me and said, "Put them on." I was mad now. There was nothing I could do to stop this either. I kicked off my trainers, pulled of my t-shirt then my sweat pants. I left my socks and jock strap on. Wayne came real close and whispered in my ear. "Lose the jock," he said. I looked back at him in shock. Again whispering in case some other guys came in. "You're fucking kidding me. There ain't no way I am working out in just shorts. No fucking way." I looked defiant. "Fine Steve. Do whatever you want. The guys are really going to enjoy that clip on Monday." Wayne started to close up the locker and head out. "Wait. OK. Fine. "Wayne came back. He stood there and watched. I stripped out of my jock. I reached for the shorts and put them on. They seemed pretty normal. It felt weird not having on anything underneath though. Then I unfolded the tank top and put that on as well. It took a while to figure it out. It was a string tank top. The front was cut down to my bellybutton. My entire chest was exposed. "Wayne, you are not serious. I can't go out there like this. Look at me." Wayne stood back and smiled. Evidently he liked what he saw. "Ready to work out buddy?"

It was still pretty early. There were only a handful of people working out. I thanked God for that. Today was leg day. We headed to the back room with the leg equipment. Another blessing. Not many guys worked their legs in this gym. They were more focused on chest and arms. We had the entire room to ourselves. I felt so self conscious in that tank top. I'm glad I was in good shape so I could carry this off but still I was showing everything. "OK buddy. Let's start with the leg press." I watched as Wayne got on the machine and did a set. "Your turn buddy". Wayne was smiling for some reason. I lied down on the machine and put my feet up on the equipment. It was then that I felt this breeze right up the crack of my ass. I quickly lowered my legs and felt down the back of my shorts. The seam was ripped for about 3-4 inches. "Wayne, I have to go change. These 'great' shorts of yours are ripped." I laughed and started to get up. Wayne put a hand on my shoulder and pushed me back down onto the machine. "You are not changing. You are working out. Now get back into position." I looked at Wayne. I knew he meant business. There were a few other guys in the room now. I didn't want to start anything there. I whispered "Fuck Wayne. What if someone sees?" Wayne was not concerned at all. "So they'll figure you ripped your shorts. Now start pressing." The set seemed to go on forever. With every press I could hear the material rip even more. Wayne was standing over me watching. The machine was aside a wall. Although Wayne had a perfect shot of my hairy hole and the ass surrounding no one else in the room would have. "Wait Steve. The position of your bench is all wrong. Let me adjust that for you." I had no idea what Wayne was doing now. I knew it wouldn't be good. He reached around and started adjusting the distance between the bench and the press making the distance much shorter and forcing me to crunch even tighter together. While he was adjusting the machine with one hand his other hand found the crack in my shorts. He started to rub my hole and the surrounding area. It was as if someone had turned on an electric probe and rubbed it against my ass. It pretty much had the same impact. My dick started to get hard. "OK buddy. Now, let's see another set." Wayne was laughing. He could see I was getting hard. My shorts started to tent up. By the time I finished the set I was at full erection. "OK buddy. Let's head over to the leg curl." "Wait Wayne. I have a little problem here." Wayne looked down and laughed. He looked around the room. Once again we had the room to ourselves. He reached down and grabbed my dick real hard. This just made matters worse. I was rock hard now. Wayne walked over to the leg curl machine. Thinking fast I reached in and tucked the head of my dick in the waist band of my shorts. Then I made sure the skimpy tank top was pulled out of my shorts. I stood up. It just about covered the problem. I went over to the leg curl machine.

Wayne was enjoying every minute of this. I stood and watched as Wayne laid face down on the machine. I couldn't help but notice how hard his ass was in his pants. I tried to look elsewhere. This wasn't helping my situation. Wayne finished his set. "Ok buddy. Your turn." I got down on the machine. At least being face down I would not have to worry about my erection for a while. I started my set. Wayne again was standing over me. After about my third lift I felt something against my hole. In shock I stopped. "Keep lifting" Wayne commanded. I continued the set. Wayne was rubbing up and down against my hole. I looked around; there was no one in the room. Then he reached under and started to rub the area right below my balls. I was in agony now. I was so hard and excited, now I was starting to pre-cum. I couldn't finish this set fast enough. I finished the set and got up. My dick head secure in the waist band of my shorts. I looked down at the small puddle of pre-cum on the bench. Wayne was already making his way to the next machine.

We continued our routine. Wayne kept tormenting me whenever he had a chance.

Usually our leg routine lasts for 45 minutes. We were already exercising for about 90 minutes this morning. "Come on Wayne. Enough is enough. We're done right?" "Yeah ok buddy. Let's hit the showers." I followed Wayne into the locker room. A lot of guys had started coming in now. I stripped out of my skimpy outfit quickly. I was glad to be rid of it. I got my towel and hit the showers. Wayne was taking his time getting changed.

⁓

Wayne was having a ball tormenting Steve. Steve had gotten so hard during the work out. What Steve didn't realize was how hard Wayne had gotten during the entire routine. Wayne had worn a jock strap and his baggy work out clothes. He could hide anything under them. Wayne waited until Steve had gone into the showers. Then he went for Steve's locker. He got out Steve's gym bag. Steve always packed clean clothes to put on after his workout. Jeans, T shirt, boots, underwear. Wayne had to act fast. Two guys had just left the locker room to go workout. He was now alone. He got Steve's underwear and hid them in a locker 3 rows down. Then he got Steve's jeans. He pulled out his pocket knife and cut a slit right up the back. Then he put the jeans and t-shirt right where he'd found them. He went into the showers to join his buddy.

⁓

It felt real good to hit the showers. Wayne had gotten me so worked up over the past hour. I rinsed off and then hit the steam room. It always felt great to have a steam after a good workout. I wrapped the towel around myself then headed in. The room was empty. A few minutes later Wayne came in. He sat down right next to me. His leg started rubbing against mine. I moved away. He just moved right next to me. Right up against me. He grabbed my hand and placed it on his crotch. He was rock hard. "Fuck Wayne. Not in here." I whispered to him. Wayne wasn't about to stop. He moved his towel aside and showed me his rod. Fuck it was huge. I couldn't take my eyes off it. I found myself staring at the length. How the veins ran along the shaft. The huge mushroom head. My dick started to get hard. Without saying a thing Wayne grabbed the back of my head and pulled me down on his dick. Even if I wanted to stop him I couldn't. Part of me didn't want to. I started sucking on his dick. It didn't take long for my own dick to get rock hard. Luckily my towel covered it. We heard someone coming and I quickly sat up. We both just leaned against the wall before he got in. The guy didn't stay long. He left shortly after. "Hey Steve ole buddy. Give me your towel." It was more a command than a request. "No way Wayne. Come on. Please." It was no use. Wayne wasn't taking no for an answer. I stood up and took my towel off. Then I sat back down again. Wayne put the towel underneath him. My dick was semi hard. Luckily it was going down. Wayne immediately pulled my head down on his dick again. It didn't take long for my dick to be standing at attention. I sucked Wayne real well. He had started to moan. I was leaking big time. It was then we heard someone coming. Again we both sat back but this time I had nothing to cover myself with. The only thing I could do was cross one leg over my knee and hope I could hide it. Wayne was chuckling under his breath. Two more guys came in. To my horror Wayne got up to leave, taking both his and my towel with him. I had to sit and wait until my erection went down before I could leave. I finally was able to head back to the showers. Wayne had left my towel on a hook outside the shower room. I showered and went to get dressed.

Wayne was already dressed and waiting for me. He sat as I got my clothes out. "Damn. I could have sworn I packed underwear," I said despondently. I couldn't find them in my bag. "I must have forgotten to pack them." I said to Wayne. "No problem buddy. Come on. Let's get going." Wayne was acting impatient. I unfolded my t shirt and put it on. I got my jeans out and started to put them on as well. "Aw Fuck!" I couldn't believe it. My jeans were ripped up the seam. "What's wrong Steve?" Wayne tried but couldn't control his smile. "You fucker" I said. "I can't believe you did this." I had no other choice. I pulled the jeans on. I could feel the opening in the back. My ass was practically hanging out. There was no way I could walk out like that. I got the string tank top and tucked it into the back of my jeans so it was hanging over the slit. Embarrassed I followed Wayne back to his car. The entire way back to Wayne's house he kept reaching under my ass and fingering my hole. I was his play toy for the weekend. That was a workout I wouldn't forget too quickly.

We pulled into Wayne's driveway. "OK Steve ole buddy. I have a full day planned for you. There are tons of chores around this house that need to get done before the girls get home. Let's get started." Wayne was heading around the back of his house and I followed him. "Ah. Wayne. There's no way I can work around here with my ass hanging out of my jeans like this. I have to go home and change. I'll be back in a few minutes." I started to head over to my place. "No Steve. No need. You'll wear a pair of my gym shorts. It's going to be a real nice day today. Pretty warm. Follow me." Wayne said. I wasn't sure what Wayne was up to but there was no use fighting him at this point. I'd just suck it up, do the chores and get this weekend over with. I followed him into his basement. "Why don't you strip out of them jeans and tee shirt? I'll be right back with the shorts." I took the jeans off then my tee shirt. I felt a little uncomfortable standing there naked waiting for Wayne to get back. I started thinking of the situation I had gotten myself into. I was under Wayne's control for the entire weekend. Having to do whatever he asked. Then my dick started getting hard. Damn thing has a mind of its own. I tried thinking of anything else before Wayne got back and saw it. Willing it to go down but nothing worked. I heard Wayne coming down the basement stairs. I stood in back of the easy chair to try and hide my problem. "OK good buddy. I have your shorts. What are you doing behind there? Come out here and try these on." Wayne stood in the middle of the basement TV room. I walked from around the chair my dick pointing straight to the ceiling. My face turned red. I reached for the shorts. "No, no no. Wait a minute. What's going on here?" Wayne started laughing again. "You are as hard as a rock. Do you like this buddy?" Wayne roared with laughter. "I think you do." Wayne calmed down and handed me the shorts. "Put these on. We've got work to do." I grabbed the shorts eager to get anything. The shorts were white. Wayne had worn them several times while we worked out. Wayne usually worked up quite a sweat during our morning work outs. If it wasn't for the lining in them they would have been see through. "Wayne. I don't have any underwear remember. You didn't bring any down. How about getting me a pair bud?" I pleaded. "Just put on the fucking shorts. We have lots of work to do." Wayne was getting aggravated. I knew they were lined so it wouldn't be that bad. I opened them up to put them on. "Fuck Wayne. You cut the lining out of 'em. I can't wear these." I prattled miserably. "I said to put the fucking shorts on. Do it now or you are going to be doing chores around here in a fucking jock strap." Wayne said with a sneer. I didn't want to test Wayne on that last suggestion. I put the shorts on. They fit. I was glad to have something on. Without the lining you could almost see through the shorts but not quite. I'm not sure what would happen if I started to sweat. I didn't want to think about that. I pulled my trainers back on as well. "OK Steve ole buddy. Let's get going." Wayne said. "Ah Wayne. A tee shirt or something? Come on buddy?" I pleaded again. "That's all you're getting and if I hear one more complaint I'm going upstairs for the jock strap." Wayne headed for the basement door. I followed Wayne out of the basement and around to the front of house. In just a pair of almost see through white shorts and a pair of trainers.

"The first task of the day is to wash my truck. You can do it right here in the driveway. I'll get you the bucket, soap and sponge." Wayne went into the garage to get the stuff I'd need. Now, although the back of both our homes were pretty private due to them backing up to the Town forest the front of the house was on a pretty busy street. My mind immediately thought of my shorts getting wet during the car wash. I was already dying inside of embarrassment. "OK buddy. Do a good job or else. You have a lot more to do so don't waste a lot of time on this chore." Wayne made his way to his front porch. He sat back in the shade with his feet up on the railing and settled in to watch the show. I started by getting the entire truck wet. Then I focused on one section at a time. There was no way around it I knew I was going to get wet. During the first section I reached over to get the front hood cleaned and pressed right up against the side of the truck. I didn't even want to look down but had to. My shorts were see through. You could see everything. I had to get this done fast. The truck was massive. I continued from section to section. Wetting the truck down. Soaping it up then rinsing it down. By the time I finished half the truck my shorts were soaked through. It looked as if I had no shorts on at all. Cars continued to drive by. It was getting towards mid morning. At one point a car of young women drove by and honked and called out to me. My face turned three shades of purple. I hurried through the second half of the truck. Wayne was nearly choking he was laughing so hard. I finally finished. "OK Wayne. Done. Can we head around back now?" Wayne took his time getting up off his chair and heading over to the truck. He walked around the truck examining it. "Get over here." He demanded. I went over to his side of the truck. "Yeah?" I stood there with my shorts still very see through. Several more cars honked as they drove by. "Do you call this clean? Huh?" He pointed to a section of the truck I missed in my speed to get the truck cleaned. "Come on Wayne. So I missed a section. I'll do it over again." I went to grab the hose but Wayne stopped me. "No. It's too late buddy. Follow me." Wayne headed around back. I followed, not sure what was coming next.

～

Wayne couldn't believe how hot and bothered he had gotten watching Steve wash the truck. Good thing Steve was so hell bent on getting that truck cleaned that he didn't even try to come over to Wayne and good thing Wayne was way back on the front porch. Steve didn't have a chance to see how hard Wayne had gotten. Fuck. Steve looked naked standing there washing the truck in the middle of daylight on a busy street. His muscles shining in the morning sun. Every hair on his ass visible through the white shorts. Wayne was certainly enjoying this. He made his way to the basement. Steve was right behind him.

—

I followed Wayne in through the basement to his office room. "Wayne come on. What's going on? This is ridiculous." I said as I walked behind him. "I told you to do a good job. You did a shit job. I don't think you are taking this very seriously. I think punishment is in order. You need to realize I mean business." Wayne said in a threatening tone. "Punishment? What the fuck Wayne. Come on please. Give me a break." I pleaded and begged with Wayne at this point but it was no use. I watched as Wayne got a bar stool and placed it in the middle of the room. "I want you to lay face down over the stool," he told me. I hesitated. "I SAID TO LAY FACE DOWN. NOW!" I laid face down over the stool. I grabbed two of the legs for support. "I hate to do this to you buddy but you clearly screwed up. You need to realize I mean business." Wayne was rummaging through his desk drawers for something. I couldn't really see because the desk was behind me. "Wayne please. I'll do a better job on the next chore. I promise." I said. "Yes buddy. You sure will." Wayne was leaning over me, his chest against my back pinning me down on the stool. He reached down and placed a handcuff around my wrist. "WHAT THE FUCK WAYNE!" I tried to get up but couldn't. Wayne was bigger than I was. He quickly reached under the stool and placed the other side of the cuff around my other wrist. Wayne got up off me. I was pinned down to the stool. My wrists cuffed under the rung. I couldn't get up. "Come on Wayne. I can't believe you are doing this." I struggled but couldn't get free. I was trapped there. "What's wrong buddy. Not comfortable?" Wayne roared with laughter. Again I could hear him searching through his desk drawers. He walked over to me. He was right behind me at this point. He grabbed the waist- band of the white shorts and pulled them down to my ankles. "Fuck Wayne. What are you doing?" I asked him beseechingly. Wayne was standing right behind me. "I told you. It's about time you realize I am serious."

—

Wayne couldn't help but stand there and look at his buddy cuffed down to the stool. Damn his ass was like two melons. He was covered in fur. His legs were like tree trunks. His back and arms bulging from the workouts they had done every morning.

Wayne got the paddle ready. He knew that those old ping pong paddles would come in handy for something someday.

—

WHACK! I didn't feel the first whack coming. "Fuck Wayne. What are you doing? WHACK! "I'm punishing you for doing a shit job on my truck." WHACK! Wayne was going at my ass with a paddle. WHACK! "Please Wayne. You can't do this." WHACK! "Oh shit" WHACK! My ass was starting to sting now. WHACK! Wayne kept at it. A regular pounding every minute or so. WHACK! "Please Wayne. You can't do this. I'll do anything for the rest of the weekend. No complaints. Honest. Just let me up."WHACK! Wayne hesitated. "OK. Anything. No complaints. We got tons of things to do."WHACK! "That was 10. Next time you screw up we are coming down here for 20. You got that?" Wayne put the paddle down but he didn't un-cuff me yet. "Wayne let me up. I promise. I'll cooperate." I could hear Wayne searching through his drawers again. Then he was standing right behind me. "I think you need a constant reminder that I am in charge. This should do it." I felt Wayne press his finger against my asshole. "Fuck Wayne. What are you doing?"Wayne didn't respond. He didn't stop either. He was working his finger into my hole. He had lubed it good before trying. "Wayne. I can't believe you are doing this. Come on buddy. You can't be serious." Wayne continued working his finger in and out of my hole. "Got to get that hole nice and loose for me buddy. You better stop fighting and start relaxing." Wayne added a second finger to the assault. I thought I was going to hit the ceiling. "FUCK WAYNE. You got your entire hand in there?" He chuckled but kept at it. Working both his fingers in and out of my hole. The pain was starting to ease. Wayne kept at it. Stretching my hole with his fingers. Then I felt the tip of something against my hole. I couldn't turn my head to see what he was doing. "Wayne. What are you doing? What is that?" Wayne continued to press whatever it was against my hole. I could feel my hole being stretched wider and wider. "It's a butt plug buddy. I want you to know for the rest of the day who is in charge. This should do the trick."Wayne continued to work the plug in my ass. "Wayne. Seriously buddy. I can't take any more. FUCK! Oh man. Pull it out NOW." I struggled against the cuffs but it was no use. Finally when I thought my ass was stretched as wide as it could my ass snapped shut around the base of the plug. "There. That shouldn't be going anywhere soon." Wayne laughed as he walked away. He came back in a few minutes and un-cuffed me. "OK stand up and pull your shorts up." Wayne was standing in front of me with his arms crossed.

"Wayne, you aren't going to keep this thing in me are you?" I gasped. "Oh yeah. You did just agree to anything with no complaints. Remember? "Wayne chuckled. "Now, let's get back to work. Follow me."

I followed Wayne out to the back yard as best I could. It was difficult walking with that massive plug in my ass. Every movement reminded me of my current situation. Wayne had a shed in the back of the yard right before the forest started. He had just received a delivery of wood for winter burning. It was piled behind the shed. "OK Steve. This wood needs to be cut into pieces that will fit into my wood burning stove in the kitchen. The axe is beside the shed. Have fun. I'll be back in an hour. This entire pile better be chopped and stacked." I picked up the axe then positioned the first log for chopping. I couldn't believe I was doing this with a plug in my ass. After the first 5 logs I was sweating like a pig. So on top of everything else my white shorts were see through again. Great. I could see Wayne on his back porch sitting in the shade with his feet up having a beer. He was enjoying this.

Wayne knew that butt plug would come in handy someday. He had been planning this for quite a while. Steve didn't know it yet but that plug had a special feature. It had a vibrating feature that could be triggered by remote control. Wayne had the remote in his hand waiting for just the right moment to turn it on.

I had been chopping wood for about 30 minutes. I was soaked with sweat and my shorts were transparent. It was then that I felt something strange happening in my ass. Almost like an electric shock. I dropped the axe. No sooner had it started then it stopped. Confused, I picked up the axe and started to chop again. Within minutes I felt it again. This time it lasted for a longer period of time. It was coming from the plug in my ass. I looked over to Wayne. He was doubled over laughing his ass off with a remote control in his hand. The fucker. The vibration was coming in waves lasting for about a minute then stopping. The effect on my dick was obvious. I had gotten a raging hard on. My shorts were tenting big time. I knew the clock was ticking. I only had about 25 minutes left and over half the pile of wood left to chop. I tried going back to work. The vibrations seemed to be getting stronger with each minute that went by. My fucking cock was dripping at this point. I had a hard time focusing on chopping wood. I knew I wasn't going to make it.

I watched out of the corner of my eye as Wayne made his way up the yard to the back of the shed. "I'm disappointed in you buddy. I told you I wanted this pile cut and stacked in an hour. You aren't even three quarters of the way there." Wayne reprimanded me. "Come on Wayne. Give me a few more minutes. I can get this done. That fucking plug in my ass is driving me crazy. The damn thing is vibrating. Shut that remote off will you!" I said. "I'm disappointed in you Steve. I thought we had a deal. You do as you are told or you receive punishment. Isn't that the deal?" I knew when I was defeated. I dropped the axe. "Yes. We have a deal. Let's get this over with." Wayne looked pleased. "Now that's the spirit. Now drop your shorts." I was shocked. I looked around. "Out here? Are you for real? Fuck Wayne." "Yes Steve. Out here. It's completely private. Now drop 'em." Wayne told me again. I was embarrassed beyond belief but knew Wayne had the final say. I dropped the soaking wet shorts to about my ankles. My dick was as hard as a rock and dripping from the vibrating plug in my ass. "Good job buddy. Now you are cooperating. Do you remember how many whacks you are getting?" I watched as Wayne pulled the paddle out from the back of his jeans. Fuck, I couldn't believe I was doing this and my dick was still rock hard. "Fuck Wayne. 5 whacks?" Wayne laughed. "No buddy. I think we said 20. Now bend over and grab your ankles." Embarrassed beyond belief I looked around again to make sure no one was watching this. It was pretty secluded this far in the back of his yard behind the shed. I bent over and grabbed my ankles. The plug still lodged deep in my ass. The vibrating had stopped. "Now, I want you to count off as I paddle your ass." WHACK! "Oh fuck......ONE. WHACK, "grrrrrrr TWO" WHACK ..." oh....fuck Wayne.... THREE" .....WHACK, WHACK, WHACK, "hmmmmmgghhh ....FOUR, FIVE, SIX." My ass was burning hot at this point. I have no idea how I got through the rest of the punishment. Wayne continued to paddle my ass. It seemed like an eternity but it was finally coming to an end............WHACK "TWENTY". "Good man. You took that with very little complaint. You are learning. Now stand up, pull your shorts up and finish chopping that wood." I stood slowly. My poor ass was red hot. The plug in my ass was no longer feeling as bad as before. I must have been getting used to it. Embarrassed and humiliated over what had just happened I picked up the axe and continued to chop the wood. Wayne had returned to his seat on the back porch. I watched every now and then between swings of the axe. He went into the house a couple of times and came out with a new beer. Damn that cold beer would go good right about now. A good 45 minutes later I had piled all the wood up against the shed. He came down to the shed just as I was finishing piling the wood. He was carrying a gym bag. "Good job Steve. It's time for a little break. You deserve it; you've been working very hard around here. Let's go. Follow me."

I followed Wayne deeper into the woods. The wooded area behind our house was a Town Forest. There were numerous trails. You had to travel pretty far in to get to the trails used most often by the public. I'd say a good 2-3 miles. We were getting close. "Wayne, where are you going? What's going on?" I wasn't sure what Wayne had planned next but I had a sinking feeling that it wasn't going to be good. "Just keep up buddy. You'll see." I was following Wayne still wearing just my white shorts and a pair of trainers. It looked as if Wayne was searching for something. We had been following one of the trails. He moved off of the path and we were now making our way through the trees. Finally he stopped in a small clearing. "Perfect." Wayne said almost to himself. "OK buddy we're here. Time for that well deserved break I promised you." We were standing under a large tree; its branches started just a foot above our heads. The branches were a good foot thick. "OK. Here's what you are going to do and you are going to follow it to the letter because I am getting tired of your complaining and whining. Any more grief from you and I'm just heading back to my office to send a few emails. You got that?" Wayne was about two inches from my face. He meant business. I was not sure where this was going. Why the fuck was my dick starting to stir again? Wayne was waiting for an answer. "ANSWER ME! Do you understand?" "Yes, yes. I understand. OK. Calm down." "Good. I'm glad we are on the same page. Now reach overhead and grab that tree branch." Confused and not sure what he was up to I did as he instructed. I was able to grab hold of it easily. Wayne reached into the gym bag and pulled out that pair of handcuffs from before. "Wayne. What are you going to do?" You could hear the fear in my voice. I didn't dare move my hands but the thought did occur to me. I knew if I gave him any more trouble he'd send that video clip out. Wayne didn't answer. He reached up and cuffed my left wrist. Then he threw the cuffs over the tree limb. He grabbed my right wrist and pulled it up to reach the cuff. He snapped it around my right wrist. I was still able to stand on the ground but I was stretching. "There. How does that feel buddy? Nothing like a good stretch to work out all those KINKS in your back." He got a chuckle out of that one. I could hear him searching through the contents of the gym bag behind me. I couldn't see what he was doing. "Wayne. What are you doing buddy? Come on. Hasn't this gone far enough?" I thought I could calmly reason with him. "I've been doing any chores you asked me to. What are you doing?" I couldn't see Wayne. He was standing behind me. "OK buddy. I'm a fair man. If you are still sporting a hard on then we keep going. If you are completely soft then we stop. I think that's fair." Just at that moment the vibrating plug in my ass came to life. It had been quiet for quite a while. I had almost forgotten it was there. My dick went rock hard immediately. Wayne came around front and grabbed my dick through my shorts. "Ha. I thought so. You are fucking loving this. Guess we continue." Wayne was laughing as he went back around to his bag. I was cursing my constantly hard dick.

Wayne came around front holding his jock strap from our work out this morning. "You know good buddy, whenever the wife is away I have a tendency of not wanting to do laundry. I've been wearing this strap for the past 4 workouts. Here, take a whiff." At that Wayne shoved the jock strap under my nose. I began to open my mouth to protest. "Fuck Wayne…hgggmmhgmmmmm" Wayne had shoved the jock strap into my complaining mouth. "There that should shut you up for a while." Wayne was laughing to himself. Then he stood in front of me and peeled off his tank top. It was thread bare from all the workouts it had been through. He used the tank top as a gag and tied it around my head holding his smelly jock strap in place in my mouth. For some reason my dick remained rock hard. "There good buddy. That should keep that strap in place." I couldn't believe what was happening to me. My wrists cuffed over a tree limb. Unable to move or get free. "OK buddy. I have some office work I have to catch up on. I'll be back in a while. Don't go anywhere." Wayne laughed his ass off at this one. He placed the remote control on the ground directly in front of me. The vibrating plug was humming away in my ass. I tried screaming into the gag but it made no difference. All the struggling I was doing only caused my wrists to cut into the cuffs. I was trapped. At his whim. I watched as he made his way out of the clearing and back to the path heading to his back yard. I was totally screwed now.

~

Wayne was hard as a rock as he made his way back to his house. The sight of Steve cuffed to that tree really got to him. He went around to his truck and headed to the gym. He didn't want to leave his buddy out there alone for too long. He knew a guy at the gym that would jump at the idea he was going to propose to him. He always worked out from Saturday noon on. Wayne had run into him one weekend in the sauna after an exceptionally long work out. The guy gave Wayne one of the best blow jobs he ever had. It was definitely worth trying to see if he was up for a little fun. It didn't take long for Wayne to find him. His luck was continuing. He pulled the guy aside and made his proposal. The guy would only agree to the plan if he could bring his workout partner along as well. Wayne shook hands on the deal and gave him instructions on where to go and when. Wayne headed back to his house.

I'm not sure how long I had been hanging there but it felt like hours. I started to imagine hearing things in the woods. Branches snapping or the rustle of leaves. I tried looking in the direction of the noise but saw nothing. Luckily I was not on a main path. I was very out of the way. No one could stumble on me by mistake. That damn vibrating plug was making me crazy. Then I heard it. A definite snap. I looked in the direction of the noise and saw two figures making their way through the woods. They had obviously veered off the main path. I tried to remain perfectly still so they couldn't hear me. I was hoping they would continue by. No chance. They made their way right towards me as if they had a fucking map or something. When they got closer I almost died. I recognized both of them from the same gym Wayne and I went to. Tony and Dan. Tony was wearing a backpack. I was totally humiliated.

"Now what have we here? Tony. Take a look at this. Looks like someone's been having some fun with you huh Steve?" I tried talking through my gag but it was no use. "Tony, look at this. Steve is handcuffed. Wow. You know Wayne told us about your kinky side. I thought he was putting us on but I guess he wasn't." I was dying inside. They thought I had a kinky side. What else had Wayne told them? Again I tried yelling into my gag but it was no use. They were real close now. One in front of me and one behind. "You know Dan I can't quite make out what he is saying can you?" "Fuck no Tony; I don't understand a thing he is saying. Hey let's see if everything else Wayne told us is true." Tony was standing behind me. I felt him grab the waistband of my shorts. He yanked them down to my ankles then took them off leaving me hanging in just my trainers. "Dan, there's something humming back here. Fuck Dan, he has a plug up his ass. Damn, Wayne wasn't kidding about this guy." They both roared with laughter. I turned about three shades of red. "Tony, he is as hard as a rock. He's even dripping he is so excited. He loves this." Dan grabbed my dick hard and started jacking on it. They both had their hands all over me at that point. Tony started feeling up my ass while Dan was working my front side. Pulling on my tits. Bighting them.

Pulling on my balls. Meanwhile Dan was pushing the butt plug in as far as it could go. They were having a ball.

~

Wayne had been waiting a safe distance away from the hanging Steve. He thought Steve had heard him approach but he remained very still. Wayne had his camcorder positioned right on Steve. He would make sure to get every shot of this scene. He watched as Tony and Dan approached. He started taping.

~

I watched as Tony took the backpack off. He moved around behind me and placed it on the ground. I couldn't see what he was doing back there. Again I tried screaming into the gag. No use. "Tony, Steve is really enjoying this. Look at the pre cum coming out of this guy. Don't worry Steve we're going to take good care of you. Your good friend Wayne told us exactly what you were into. We're going to make sure we get into everything you enjoy. Don't worry." I tried screaming NOOOOOOO into the gag but it didn't quite come out that way. Tony came around front totally naked and with a leather strap in his hands but it wasn't just a strap. It had chains attached to it. He grabbed my balls and pulled on them. Now my balls are pretty good sized and hang low. There was a lot to grab. I watched as he wrapped the leather around my balls. The chains hung below the leather. Once secured he was able to pull on the chain and thus torture my poor balls. They took turns pulling on my balls. They added a length of chain to the ball stretcher and attached the other end to a low lying tree limb. They made sure the chain was nice and tight pulling my balls down and away from my body. The screams into my gag made no impact on these two. "Damn Tony you do good work. Look at the stretch on those balls. His dick is even harder than before. He loves this." It was Dan's turn. He disappeared behind me. I could hear him going through the backpack. He came back totally naked with a pair of clamps connected by a chain. I wasn't exactly sure what they were for but I was soon to find out. I watched in horror as he pulled my right nipple away from my chest. He put the first clamp around my nipple. I went crazy. The pain shot through my nipple and chest. I screamed into the gag. He then clamped my left nipple. I couldn't believe the pain at first. I was screaming non-stop. The pain soon gave way to this very erotic feeling. "Good job Dan. Wayne told me this was one of his favorites. You love this Steve don't you?" All

I could do was look at him in silence.

Tony and Dan reached into the backpack again. This time they stayed behind me. I felt one of them pull my butt plug out. At that point it had been in me for several hours. It hurt like hell coming out. My hole wasn't empty for long though. I felt the head of another toy against my hole. I wasn't sure what it was but it was bigger than the plug. Again I screamed into the gag. "Damn Tony. Look at his ass suck up that dildo. It's the biggest one we brought. Wayne had warned us that Steve was used to taking very large toys. He was right. Next time we'll have to get larger ones." Next time I thought to myself. Not if I can help it. There'll be no next time. The dildo was deep in my ass. Tony and Dan tied a leather strap around the base and then wrapped it around my hips securing the dildo in place. It wasn't going anywhere. Again both Tony and Dan had their hands all over me. They were taking turns sucking on my dick. It was driving me crazy. Finally I was so close I started to moan. They knew it was coming. I had such an explosive orgasm it hit the tree in front of me. They each started jacking off. They both came at the same time and covered me with their cum. Tony and Dan started taking the toys off me. Removed the dildo and replaced the butt plug. They took off the tit clamps and the ball stretcher. They dressed and left me just as they found me. Except this time I was totally naked. Helpless, naked, and in Wayne's total control.

The two men had worked on Steve for several hours. Wayne had gotten every minute of the action. This would add a little insurance to his future blackmailing efforts against Steve. He could also use it on Tony and Dan he thought fiendishly. They would be forced to come back for a repeat.

I'm not sure if I started to fall asleep. It was dark by the time Wayne came back for me. He took me down from the tree limb but cuffed my hands behind my back. I was too weak to resist. Then he grabbed me by the balls and pulled me back to the path that led to his house. We stopped at his back porch. "OK buddy. You did real well today. You behave yourself tomorrow and that video clip will be our little secret." Wayne chuckled under his breath. "Tomorrow? Fuck Wayne. There ain't no way I can take another day of this." "Oh you will buddy. You will. Now bend over." I bent over obediently. Wayne pulled the plug from my ass. I made my way naked back to my house. It was close to midnight. I don't even remember hitting the pillow that night.

Sunday

I woke to someone ringing the front doorbell repeatedly. I looked at the clock; it was only 4:45. Just then I remembered it was time for the gym. I grabbed a towel from the bathroom, wrapped it around myself and went to answer the front door. It was Wayne. "Come on buddy. Time for our workout." Wayne said. "Aw Wayne, I am beat from the workout you gave me yesterday. How about skipping today?" I suggested. "No chance Steve. We work out every morning. Let's get going." Wayne admonished me. I knew it was no use. I was Wayne's play toy for the weekend. "OK fine. Let me get my stuff." I started to head back into the house but Wayne grabbed my arm. "No time for that man. You can change on the way. Come on. Let's go." Wayne pulled me out of the doorway and slammed it shut behind me. Both our doors work the same. You close the door and it locks automatically. I was now locked out in a fucking towel. Wayne pulled me by the arm down the front walk. "Wayne. I'm in a fucking towel here. What the fuck!" I prattled. "Stop your whining. I have your gym clothes in the truck. Get in." Wayne ordered. I got into the truck in just my towel. Wayne got in the drivers side and took off. While driving he reached around back and handed me my outfit for the day. The same string tank top from yesterday but a different pair of shorts. Thank God. I put the tank top on. Then I opened the shorts. "Ah. Wayne. This is a pair of boxer brief underwear. I can't wear these to the gym." "Sure you can.

I saw a guy wearing these just the other day. Put them on." I opened the towel and put the briefs on. If I get hard in these everyone will see everything. We pulled up to the gym. Embarrassed as hell I walked in through the front reception area. I felt like everyone was staring as I walked past. Wayne was already in his gym clothes. I followed him into the locker room. He threw his bag into the locker then we both hit the cardio room.

Sunday was always Cardio day. We ran for about 45 minutes then did abs work. I started on the treadmill but had a hard time reaching my normal speed. I was still sore from yesterday. Wayne was right beside me. I was curious as to why he hadn't tried anything yet. Other than the skimpy outfit he wasn't really tormenting me today. Perhaps he was feeling sorry for me. Then Tony and Dan came in. They were never there this early on a Sunday. I knew something was up. I tried not to look their way. I was hoping they would ignore me. No chance of that happening. They came right over to me. "Hey Steve. Good seeing you again. Have a good day yesterday?" They both looked at each other and laughed. They said a few things to Wayne that I couldn't hear. Then all three of them looked over to me. I felt like I was on the treadmill naked. It felt as though they were looking right through me. They made their way over to the weight room for their work out. Wayne and I finished up and hit the locker room. Just by coincidence Tony and Dan were in the locker room at the same time. I stripped out of my clothes, grabbed a towel and hit the steam room. Nothing like a good steam right after a run. I was soon followed by Tony, Dan and Wayne. Wayne was the last one in. Wayne shut the light off and locked the door after him. I knew something was up. "Wayne. What are you doing? No way Wayne. Not here. Not now." Tony and Dan had sat down on either side of me. They each took a hold of one of my arms. They were pretty built. "Come on Wayne. Fuck. No way." Wayne took my towel and stripped it off of me. Then Tony and Dan stood me up, turned me around and forced me to bend over by punching me in the gut. I was winded but not hurt. They held me down in this position. I felt Wayne behind me. He worked a handful of lube into my hole. I could see he was already rock hard. I felt his dick head against my hole. With one shove he pushed the entire length into my ass. I tried screaming out but Dan had his hand over my mouth. Wayne fucked me good. Pounding into my ass. Then he pulled out and switched places with Tony. Tony positioned himself against my hole and dove right in. All three guys took their turns with my ass. They would pound my ass for a few minutes then switch. They made three rotations then couldn't hold back any longer. They came all at once all over my back. They turned on the light, unlocked the door and made their way to the shower. They didn't even leave me a towel. I sat in the steam and tried to recover. I was so hard I jacked off all over myself. I hit the shower covered in cum.

I finished showering, grabbed another towel and got back to my locker. Just then I realized that I didn't have any clothes to change into. Wayne and the others had already changed and left. I put my sweat soaked gym clothes back on and met Wayne out at his truck. "Have a good workout Steve ole buddy?" Wayne chuckled. I sat there and didn't say a word. I'm glad he didn't know I jacked off in the shower over the scene we just had. We headed home. This weekend from hell was almost over.

We pulled into Wayne's driveway. "Well Steve the girls will be home in a couple of hours. Looks like our weekend is coming to an end. I have one more chore for you to do before they get here." "Wayne, you have put me through hell this weekend. What else could you ask of me?" I asked him. "Come on buddy. A deal was a deal. You've really held up your end of the deal as well. I'd hate for it to fall apart at the last minute wouldn't you? Hmmm?" I knew the girls would be home soon. It would soon be over with. "Fine. What next?" "That's better. Follow me." I followed Wayne around back to the basement and went inside after him. We went into his basement office. "OK buddy. Your final task will be to cut my lawn first then your lawn. Then you are done." Well. That didn't seem so bad. I definitely had to get mine done anyway. "OK Wayne. What's the catch?" I didn't trust him at this point. "Steve. Catch? You hurt my feelings. All I ask is that you change into these?" He held up the white gym shorts from yesterday. "Hell. Fine. Give them to me." I reached for them. "Wait. There is more." Wayne smiled a devilish grin as he tossed me the vibrating butt plug. "I want this in you." "Fuck Wayne. Again?. Aw shit. Come on. Do I have to?" I asked. "No buddy. You don't have to do it at all." Wayne headed over to his computer and turned it on. "Hold on a second buddy. I have a few e-mails I've been meaning to send all weekend." "Fuck. NO. Ok. You win." "That's better Steve ole buddy. Now strip out of them wet gym clothes." Wayne stood there and watched as I peeled off the tank top and took off the underwear. Again I was standing there in just my trainers. I started to bend over but Wayne stopped me. "No buddy. I ain't putting this in you. You are going to insert it into yourself." Wayne took a seat at his desk chair and leaned back with his feet on the edge of the desk. "Wayne, you aren't serious. There's no way I can shove that up my own ass." Wayne just turned around and opened his email. "OK OK. FINE." Wayne tossed me the tube of lube. I couldn't believe I was doing this.

I greased up the butt plug. Then I put about a handful of lube on my ass. It was still sore from the pounding I got at the gym. I placed the edge of the plug against my hole but had a hard time getting it in. "Use the floor as leverage buddy." Embarrassed I got down on my knees with the end of the plug against the floor. Wayne jumped down off the desk chair and positioned himself right behind me for a good view. Using the floor as leverage I pushed against the plug until the monster was half way up my hole. It didn't hurt as bad as yesterday. I must be getting used to it. My ass felt like an entire fist was being pushed up inside it. Just when I didn't think I could take much more my hole snapped shut around its base. It was in. Wayne had enjoyed the show. He was grabbing at his dick through his pants. "OK buddy. Get those shorts on. You have some lawn to cut."

I followed Wayne out to the shed, started up his mower and got to cutting his lawn. Wayne sat back on the porch with his feet up watching. Every few minutes or so he would turn the vibrator on just so I remembered who was in charge. He was having a blast. When I finished his lawn I put his mower away and then went to my yard to get mine out. Wayne moved to my back porch. Same position. Nice and relaxed. Feet up. I was really focusing on the yard. I wanted to get this done so I could remove this damn plug. My dick had been hard in my shorts the entire time I was cutting. Finally I realized Wayne was not on the back porch. I wasn't sure where he had gone. The vibrator hadn't gone off in a while either. I kept cutting. Then that damn vibrator went off all of a sudden. I turned back to the porch to give Wayne an evil look and my heart jumped into my throat. The girls had returned and were sitting on the back porch next to Wayne. Wayne had a smile from ear to ear. My wife waved to me and I waved back. Wayne obviously had the remote in his damned pocket. He kept turning it from low to medium. Driving me absolutely crazy with it. I finished cutting my lawn and put the mower away. Wayne shut the vibrator off as soon as I got near the back porch. There was no hiding my erection in my shorts. Nor was there hiding how transparent the shorts were. My wife didn't say anything but she gave me that look that said we will discuss your choice of outfits later. The girls said their goodbyes and went into the house. I stayed back with Wayne.

"So buddy. You really cooperated this weekend. That was smart of you. That clip remains our little secret." "Wayne, you have to promise you won't ever show anyone. Right?" Wayne didn't answer. "Wayne, come on. We had a deal right?" "You know good buddy. I'm thinking you owe me one more weekend of doing my bidding." I knew he had me. There wasn't much I could do. Luckily the girls had no other weekends away planned for a while. "Wayne, too bad the girls are done with their weekends away." I almost laughed as I said, "My wife will be keeping me busy for the next dozen or so weekends." I slapped him on the back and headed for my house. The girls were just coming out again. Wayne and his wife heading back to their place. My wife called to Wayne. "So Wayne. You and Steve are going on that camping trip next weekend? Steve hadn't even mentioned it but you guys deserve it after all the work you got done around here. Plus it was so nice of you two to let us go to Vegas." She waved at Wayne and his wife and went into the house. I stared at Wayne. He let his wife go into the house first then called over to me. "Looking forward to our camping trip next weekend buddy. Should be fun." He grabbed his crotch quickly without his wife seeing. I stood there with a look of shock on my face. Camping trip! Man was I screwed.

ABOUT THE EDITOR

Christopher Trevor was born in July 1963 and grew up in New York City. As soon as he was old enough to know how he began writing fiction and has been writing gay erotic/fetish stories for the past ten to twelve years at this point. He became an avid reader as well from the time he knew how and reads everything from fiction, to non-fiction to biographies of interesting and unusual people, people who have made a difference or who have paved the way for others. Christopher attributes his writing artistic inspiration to artists such as Etienne, Tom of Finland, Tagame, The Hun, and most notably Joe T, who Christopher has had the pleasure of speaking with and even meeting over the last few

years. Christopher states, "Joe T encouraged me to write about my fetish because I was embarrassed about it at the time. Joe T said that when we are embarrassed about something that makes it even more enticing somehow." Christopher totally agreed and never stopped writing in this genre. Erotic writers who inspired Christopher Trevor were: Tom Shaw (author of "That Day at the Quarry), C.S. White (author of Big Sur), Larry Townsend (author of countless erotic novels), and Mason Powell (author of the classic story "The Brig.")

Christopher discovered that not only did he enjoy writing erotic tales but that after his first bondage experience he had a genuine flair for it. Writing to erotic oriented magazines about his first bondage experience truly opened the floodgates for Christopher where this style of writing is concerned. Christopher thanks the handsome and muscular "Greg" for that experience way back in time. Christopher took "Creative Writing" courses every semester during his high school years and while other friends of his stopped writing what they loved to write about as time went on Christopher never let a day go by when he didn't write something... "I feel that if I don't write every day I will die," Christopher has said many times over.

Foot fetish stories and all things related; spanking fetish, erotic shaving, muscle bondage, tickle torture, and hardcore stories are just a few of the areas of gay eroticism that Christopher enjoys writing about and inspiring in others as well. As one internet buddy said to Christopher where the black socks fetish is concerned, "Until I started talking with you I never gave a thought to my socks when I got dressed for work in the morning. Now when I pull my dress socks on every morning I get a chill up my spine."

Christopher is proud of the erotic effect he has on people...

Christopher Trevor is also the author of:

The Executive Guide to Foot Fetishism and Office Discipline

1-887895-36-1

Executive Ties That Bind
1-887895-37-X

Don't! Stop! That Tickles!
1-887895-31-0

The Taming of Dominick
1-887895-45-0

Timmy and The Hong Kong Tailor
> 1-887895-30-2

Love, Torture and Redemption
> 1-887895-32-9

Timmys Ticklish Trials
> 978-1-887895-74-3

The Gym Instructor
> 978-1-887895-44-6

Milked
> 978-1-887895-66-8

Erotic Street Blues
> 978-1-887895-97-2

The Abusive Wager
> 978-1-887895-04-0

Terry's Appointment and Other Tickling Stories
> 978-1-934625-08-8

The Military File
> 978-1-934625-21-7

Quirks
> 978-1-934625-24-8

Timmy and the Evil Dr. Vonvellicator
> 978-1-934625-42-2

Look for them where you bought this book or Goodboner.com.

www.ingramcontent.com/pod-product-compliance
Lightning Source LLC
Chambersburg PA
CBHW071223260626
47162CB00004B/1400